VIETNAM JOURNAL

DON LOMAX
STORY AND ART

CLEM ROBINS
LETTERING

BOB LARKIN
COVER

HILARY HUGHES
DWIGHT JON ZIMMERMAN
EDITORS

BYRON PREISS
SERIES EDITOR

ibooks graphic novels
DISTRIBUTED BY SIMON AND SCHUSTER

To those we left behind

An ibooks, inc. Graphic Novel

Ibooks, inc.
24 West 25th Street
New York, NY 10010

The ibooks World Wide Web Site address is:
http://www.ibooks.net

Cover Design: Mike Rivilis

ISBN: 0-7434-5894-X

10 9 8 7 6 5 4 3 2 1

INTRODUCTION

The ten thousand day conflict that was the Vietnam War was a wrenching experience whose traumatic effect on the United States was exceeded only by that of the American Civil War one hundred years earlier.

America's reconciliation with the only war it has lost has been aided, impeded, and diverted by the creative outpouring from Hollywood and literature. To date the best books on the subject, including such fact-based accounts as *Chickenhawk, A Bright Shining Lie,* and *We Were Soldiers Once . . . And Young,* and the Vietnam novels of W. E. B. Griffin, have almost exclusively been those produced by people who experienced the war firsthand.

Don Lomax was one such individual. Drafted into the Army in 1965, he went to Vietnam in 1966. While off duty he began taking notes and making sketches of what he heard and saw. This material and his experiences ultimately found a voice in the stories that make up *Vietnam Journal.* Though a work of fiction, the stories resonate with the truth that comes from someone who has felt the heat, the anger, the fear, the helplessness, hopelessness, relief, sadness, emptiness, and guilt of being stationed in Vietnam . . . and surviving.

Lomax's art does not possess glamorous exaggeration that is the style of most graphic story illustration in the United States. His style is understated and gritty, like dirt under the fingernails. This lack of exaggeration is one of his art's greatest strengths. The violent death it depicts is visceral and disturbing, unlike the romanticized and ornately choreographed fight scenes that are the stock in trade of a typical superhero's adventures.

Lomax's narrator and participant in *Vietnam Journal* is journalist Scott "Journal" Neithammer who arrives in Vietnam expecting to write about body counts and the winning of hearts and minds. But he very quickly discovers that the real story lies elsewhere—with the grunts "humpin' the boonies," and fighting a war that was becoming more senseless and futile with each passing day.

Lomax left a part of himself in Vietnam, brought a part of Vietnam back with him, and in *Vietnam Journal* has given us both. *Vietnam Journal* is a soldier's story told without remorse or rancor. Told honestly. Told well.

Dwight Jon Zimmerman
Editor

HOPE THIS TYPEWRITER OF YOURS AIN'T ELECTRIC. ELECTRICITY IS KINDA SPORADIC UP THERE. "CHARLIE" SABOTAGES THE GENERATORS EV'RY NOW AND AGAIN. JUST HARASSMENT.

RICE PADDIES STRETCHED OUT BELOW US LIKE SHINY, SILVER POSTAGE STAMPS AGAINST A BACKGROUND OF GREEN VELVET, UNTIL THE ROUGH CENTRAL HIGHLANDS REPLACED THE FARM LANDS.

WE MAY DRAW FIRE WHEN WE LAND. THE JUNGLE IS SO THICK, WE CAN'T RUN CHARLIE OFF.

THEY'RE SUPPOSED TO *DEFOLIATE* SOON. THAT'LL BE A BLESSING.

WE MAY TOUCH DOWN KINDA HARD. GOTTA GET OUTTA HERE IN A HURRY. THE SECOND WE'RE DOWN, YOU GET YOUR OLIVE-DRAB ASS OUT THAT DOOR, UNDERSTAND?

MY BY-LINE READS: SCOTT NEITHAMMER, BUT THE TROOPS CALL ME "JOURNAL."

BEFORE I GOT TO SOUTHEAST ASIA AS A WAR CORRESPONDENT, I EXPECTED MY FEATURES TO READ LIKE THE REST...

WE'LL GET AS CLOSE TO THE COMPOUND'S PERIMETER AS POSSIBLE. JUST SCURRY ON IN THERE, YOU'LL BE FINE.

INTERVIEWS WITH GENERALS, TACTICAL STRATEGIES, COOPERATIVE CAMPAIGNS AGAINST COMMUNIST INSURGENTS, AND BODY COUNTS.

Y'ALL KEEP YER HEAD DOWN-- I'LL BE LAYING DOWN FIRE ALONG THE TREE LINE!

I UNDERSTAND.

FOLLOW ME, SIR. I'LL SHOW YOU WHERE TO STOW YOUR GEAR. HOW LONG HAVE YOU BEEN INCOUNTRY?

ABOUT FOUR HOURS.

OUTSTANDING. YOU CAN HAVE THIS COT FOR THE TIME BEING. IT BELONGED TO A SHAVETAIL WHO WENT HOME IN A BAG LAST WEEK.

WONDERFUL.

I WOULD SUGGEST YOU GET ALL THE SLEEP YOU CAN BEFORE SUNDOWN, 'CAUSE THAT'S WHEN THE FIRE- WORKS START--AND, SON, HAVE WE GOT A WAR FOR YOU!

NEITHAMMER

LOOKS LIKE YOU TOOK A ROUND IN THE TYPEWRITER, HUH?

LOOKS LIKE? DAMN!

NEITHAMMER

LOOKS LIKE ABOUT A DOZEN OF YER LETTERS ARE GONE --CAPITALS AND LOWER CASE. HOPE YOU WERE PLANNING TO WRITE SHORT STORIES.

HMM...

LISTEN, YOU COULD PROBABLY BORROW ONE FROM QUARTER- MASTER SUPPLY.

IT'S THE FIRST TENT PAST THE MOTOR POOL. YOU CAN'T MISS IT.

THANKS.

THERE WAS A WEIRD UNREALITY ABOUT THE WHOLE COUNTRY. I FELT IT THE MOMENT I LANDED. IT SEEMED LIKE EVERYONE WAS TRYING TO CONDUCT "BUSINESS AS USUAL" IN AN INSANE SITUATION.

I WONDERED HOW LONG IT WOULD TAKE ME TO BECOME AS NUTS AS EVERYONE ELSE....AND WOULD I KNOW IT WHEN IT HAPPENED?

THERE HE IS! GET BACK, STAY DOWN!

WHA?

WHAT ARE YOU TALKING ABOUT, LIEUTENANT? HE'S JUST A KID.

DAMN IT, HE HEARD YOU!

DAMN IT! DAMN IT! *DAMN IT!*

YOU SCARED HIM. HE'S RUNNING AWAY. *WHAT?*

NO, *NO!* HE'S JUST A KID!!!

TONG

I WAS INVITED TO BATTALION FOR DINNER WITH THE BRASS, BUT I BEGGED OFF, USING JET LAG AS AN EXCUSE. INSTEAD, I WENT TO MESS WITH THE COMPANY, HOPING TO SEE LT. GRIMES.

NO CREDIT

OVER HERE, SIR. YOU'RE WELCOME TO JOIN US. FEELIN' SOME BETTER?

THANKS, SERGEANT. HAVE YOU SEEN LT. GRIMES?

GONE, SIR.

WHAT DO YOU MEAN "GONE?"

GONE. FINI. OUT OF HERE. TRANS-FERRED.

I DON'T UNDER-STAND.

SIMPLE--LT. GRIMES IS SLIPPING OVER THE EDGE, SO BEFORE HE GOES COMPLETELY SCHIZO, THEY REASSIGN HIM. TYPICAL--DON'T FIX IT, PASS IT ALONG.

YESSIR, THAT'S WHY WE'RE HERE.

WHY? WHY DO YOU THINK YOU'RE HERE?

THEY SAY IT'S GOT SOME-THING TO DO WITH DOMI-NOES...

EXACTLY. WE'RE HERE TO STEM THE RELENTLESS COMMUNIST THREAT TO FREE PEOPLES EVERYWHERE.

THAT'S RIGHT. WE'LL FREE 'EM EVEN IF WE HAVE TO KILL EVERY ONE OF THEM TO DO IT!

MR. NEITHAMMER...

CALL ME "JOURNAL," EVERYONE DOES.

I'M THE SUPPLY SERGEANT. THAT'S A PRETTY BEAT-UP OLD FIELD JACKET YOU'RE WEARING. STOP BY SUPPLY AND TRADE IT IN FOR A NEW ONE.

NO, THANKS. THE COAT'S GOT SENTIMENTAL VALUE. I MADE A PROMISE TO A YOUNG SOLDIER BACK IN THE STATES THE DAY I LEFT--

YOU MUST HAVE BEEN CLOSE FRIENDS.

NOT REALLY. I ONLY KNEW HIM A FEW MINUTES. YOU WANT TO HEAR ABOUT IT?

IF YOU DON'T MIND...WE'RE KINDA STARVED FOR ENTERTAINMENT AROUND HERE.

YEAH, WE STILL GOT A COUPLA HOURS BEFORE OUR NIGHTLY EXCURSION INTO *THE TWILIGHT ZONE*.

AS FAR BACK AS I KNOW, THE HISTORY OF THIS JACKET STARTS WITH A SSGT. AMOS KAUER. HE WAS BETWEEN TOURS IN VIET NAM, ON LEAVE IN CHICAGO. THINGS WERE HEATING UP BETWEEN THE POLICE AND THE ANTI-WAR DEMONSTRATORS...

KAUER HAD AVOIDED THE MARAUDING GROUPS OF PROTESTERS UNTIL...

THE SIGHT WAS TOO MUCH FOR HIM!

AAAH!

OOF!

WHAP!

NOW YOU, YOU LITTLE...

DAMNIT!

KAUER'S FIRST USE FOR THE JACKET WAS TO SMOTHER THE FLAMES AND SAVE THE FLAG.

KAUER BROUGHT THE JACKET BACK TO 'NAM. MAYBE HE FELT THE JACKET HAD BEEN SOILED BY THOSE TRAITORS AND NEEDED TO BE CLEANSED IN BATTLE.

THE SISTERS AT THE ORPHANAGE TOOK THE BABY WITH GRACIOUS SMILES AND BOWS, BUT BLAKE KNEW THEY NEEDED ANOTHER MOUTH TO FEED AS MUCH AS THEY NEEDED THE WAR.

G.I., G.I.! YOU LEAVE YOUR COAT!

WHAT? OH NO, THAT'S NOT MI--

IT WAS SOMEONE ELSE'S--

O.K., O.K., I'LL TAKE IT. THANK YOU.

KAUER HAD TOLD THE STORY OF THE FIELD JACKET OVER BEERS ONE EVENING. NOW BLAKE WORE IT IN KAUER'S MEMORY.

WEIRD! I'VE HEARD OF SUPERSTITIOUS ATTACHMENTS TO DUMB THINGS BEFORE, BUT A FIELD JACKET?

LEMME FRESHEN YER CUP, JOURNAL.

IT GETS WEIRDER. SIX WEEKS LATER, BLAKE FOUND HIMSELF ON A FLUSH 'N' FRAG ABOUT FIFTEEN KLICKS WEST OF *BONG SON.*

BLAKE-- *BLAKE!* JESUS H. CHRIST, BLAKE, I'VE TRIPPED A MINE!

CLICK!

THE SMOKE DIED AND THE GREEN MAT OF JUNGLE CLOSED AROUND THEM. IT WAS THREE DAYS BEFORE THEY WERE FOUND.

IT'S THIEL'S MAGIC JACKET-- IT SAVED MY LIFE!

RIGHT, SURE.

AMAZING! AFTER THREE DAYS I WOULD EXPECT THIS LEG TO BE INFECTED--EVEN GANGRENOUS. BUT THERE IS NO SIGN OF SWELLING WHAT-SOEVER! YOU'RE A VERY LUCKY MAN!

NO, REALLY, THE JACKET SAVED MY LIFE!

RUMORS SPREAD. BEFORE LONG, THAT FIELD JACKET COULD PROTECT ANYBODY FROM ANYTHING, FROM A HANGNAIL TO A FULL BURST FROM AN AK-47.

IS THAT IT, IS THAT THE JACKET?

LET IT GO, KELLY, LET IT GO.

THE REMAINDER OF THIEL'S TOUR OF DUTY WAS UNEVENTFUL, THEN, TWO NIGHTS BEFORE HE WAS TO ROTATE BACK TO THE WORLD--

SO, WHATCHA GONNA DO WITH THE JACKET, THIEL?

I'VE BEEN GIVIN' IT A LOT OF THOUGHT. LIKE, I THOUGHT I'D PICK OUT THE MOST SORROWFUL PIECE OF OLIVE DRAB DUNG IN THE WHOLE BATTALION, YOU KNOW, GIVE THE JACKET A REAL WORKOUT.

THAT DESCRIPTION CAN FIT ONLY ONE PERSON--

SATTERWHITE!

AFFIRMATIVE!

IF THE JACKET CAN KEEP THIS *ALKY* ALIVE, IT *TRULY* WILL BE A MIRACLE.

ROGER.

THIEL

UH?

WHITE

US

≈SIGH≈...

ENLISTED MENS CLUB

4 A.M.

INCOMIN'!

TA-BAM!

NO, DAMN IT, *NO!* I'M TOO *SHORT* FOR THIS!

THIEL FELT NAKED!

THE JACKET! MY GOD, I GAVE AWAY THE JACKET!

CHING!

DADABAP

WHERE'S SATTERWHITE? HAVE YOU SEEN HIM? DAMN IT, ANSWER ME!

WHA...?

BABA BAP

GET THAT .50 SET UP BY THE COMMO BUNKER. CHARLIE'S BREACHED THE WIRE!

THE SAPPERS WERE REPELLED--

I KNEW WHEN I HEARD THE FIRST ROCKET THAT I WAS GONNA DIE WITHOUT THE JACKET. I *KNEW.*

JACKET, MY ASS. IF HE'D TAKEN COVER INSTEAD OF RUNNING AROUND LIKE A LUNATIC, HE'D STILL BE FINE.

SATTERWHITE WAS NOT SURE WHAT HAD JUST HAPPENED. BUT HE DID KNOW THAT THE JACKET WAS SOMEHOW SIGNIFICANT.

THREE WEEKS LATER, IN A BAR ON ONE OF **DA NANG'S** FILTHY BACK STREETS, SATTERWHITE SAT CATATONIC. HIS ALCOHOL-SODDEN BRAIN WAS A COMPLETE BLANK.

SO, HOW LONG HAS HE BEEN HERE?

I DUNNO. HE WAS SITTING THERE JUST LIKE THAT WHEN I CAME IN AN HOUR AGO!

LOOK, I GOTTA GO OVER TO THE MAIN P.X. IF HE'S STILL HERE WHEN WE COME BACK, WE CAN THROW HIM IN THE BACK OF THE TRUCK.

I DUNNO, THERE'S BEEN A LOT OF TROUBLE AROUND HERE LATELY.

WELL, TOO BAD! I AIN'T HIS MOMMA AND I AIN'T GONNA BABY-SIT HIM.

SATTERWHITE WAS SHIPPED TO THE DETOX CENTER AT **CAM RANH BAY.** AFTER SIX WEEKS, HE WAS SCHEDULED TO RETURN TO THE STATES FOR FURTHER TREATMENT.

GOOD LUCK, SON.

THANKS, DOC. I HAVE A LONG WAY TO GO, BUT I FEEL DEEP DOWN I CAN LICK THIS THING.

OFFICE

CAM RAHN BA... MEDICAL CENTER

MILITARY POLICE

SATTERWHITE WAS RETURNED WITH A COMPANY OF TROOPS IN TRANSIT TO FT. BENNING FOR AIRBORNE TRAINING. HE WAS UNEASY FLYING, BUT WEARING THE FIELD JACKET HELPED HIM.

US ARMY

I WAS COVERING AN ANTI-WAR DEMONSTRATION AT THE AIRPORT AS ONE OF MY LAST OFFICIAL ASSIGNMENTS BEFORE MY PLANE LEFT FOR VIETNAM, WHEN SATTERWHITE'S PLANE TAXIED INTO THE MILITARY DEBARK ZONE.

HELL NO! WE WON'T GO!

STOP BOMBING BABIES

NO MORE WAR

THE CROWD WAS ONE OF THE UGLIEST I HAD EVER SEEN! THE SIGHT OF THAT MANY COMBAT TROOPS AT ONE TIME CAUSED THEM TO EXPLODE!

TAKEN BY SURPRISE, THE HANDFUL OF POLICE ORDERED TO GUARD THE SECURITY FENCE WERE SPREAD TOO THIN TO DO ANY APPRECIABLE GOOD.

LOVE

NO MORE WAR

PEACE

MAKE LOVE NOT WAR

ALL RIGHT, PEOPLE, LISTEN UP. WE'RE NOT GOING TO STOOP TO THEIR LEVEL. FALL IN, COLUMNS OF TWOS--

EYES FRONT, PEOPLE.

CLUNK!

BUT IT WAS SATTERWHITE WHO FELL UNDER THE HAIL OF STONES!

WHEN I FINALLY GOT THROUGH THE CROWD TO HIS SIDE, HE LAY ON THE TARMAC WITH A LOOK OF TOTAL ASTONISHMENT ON HIS FACE.

CAPTAIN, YOU'D BEST GET YOUR PEOPLE OUT OF HERE BEFORE THIS THING TURNS INTO A FULL-SCALE RIOT! THE AMBULANCE IS ON ITS WAY.

I KEPT HIM TALKING, HOPING HE'D STAY CONSCIOUS UNTIL THE AMBULANCE ARRIVED. HE TOLD ME THE STORY OF THE JACKET, EXPLAINING HOW EVERY TEAR, HOLE, AND STAIN ON THE TATTERED COAT WAS AN INDIVIDUAL BADGE OF COURAGE.

HE DIED BEFORE THE AMBULANCE COULD ARRIVE, BUT BEFORE HE PASSED AWAY, HE ASKED ME TO TAKE THE JACKET BACK TO 'NAM SO IT WOULD BE ABLE TO FULFILL ITS DESTINY AGAIN.

REST IN PEACE, SON.

SO YOU SEE, THIS OLD FIELD JACKET IS A KIND OF *TRADITION.*

LET ME GET THIS STRAIGHT--

SSGT. KAUER KILLED AN INNOCENT WOMAN, LEAVING HER BABY AN ORPHAN--

BLAKE GETS HIS LEGS WASTED OFF--THIEL GETS HIS ASS BLOWN AWAY BECAUSE HE GAVE THE JACKET AWAY--AN' OL' SATTERWHITE, THE DRUNK, GETS CLEAR BACK TO THE WORLD BEFORE HAVING HIS SHELL CRACKED ON HIS HOME TURF.

INCOMIN' !!! HIT THE DECK!!

WHA'?

HERE WE GO, IT'S TIME TO ROCK 'N' ROLL!

KABOOOOM!

RIGHT ON TIME!

CHA-CLACK

ANYWAY, BACK TO THE SUBJECT. YOU SEEM TO THINK THAT LUCK IS CONNECTED WITH THAT JACKET--

IF THERE IS, IT'S ALL *BAD,* THINK ABOUT IT.

"THE WARMING SUN EASED SOME OF THE KNOTS OUT OF MY GUTS-- BUT NOT MANY. THE OLD FEELINGS WERE BACK--FEELINGS IMPOSSIBLE TO DESCRIBE UNLESS YOU'VE EXPERIENCED WAR."

FAIRLY EASY NIGHT--CHARLIE DON'T LIKE TO TRADE SMALL ARMS FIRE SINCE WE GOT THE .50 CAL BROWNINGS.

YEAH, HE KNOWS IF WE GET PISSED WE'LL HEAT UP THE OL' FRIGIDAIRE.

"MY FIRST EXPERIENCE WITH WAR WAS AS A COMBAT SOLDIER IN KOREA IN '51."

HOW MANY HEAVY MACHINE GUNS DO YOU HAVE?

TWO BROWNINGS--TWO MORE PROMISED--HALF A DOZEN M-60'S, TWO 81 MM MORTARS --AND A BATTERY OF 105'S AT THE ARTILLERY CO. 'BOUT HALF MILE DOWN THE ROAD.

"I THOUGHT I'D PUT THOSE FEELINGS TO REST 16 YEARS BEFORE."

ALL IN ALL, WE HAVE THE POTENTIAL TO RAIN FIRE DOWN ON CHARLIE'S GOOK ASS IF WE HAVE TO. THAT KEEPS HIM RIGHTEOUS.

SO WHAT'S THE PROCEDURE NOW?

THE DAY WATCH RELIEVES US AT 0600, THEN I ENTERTAIN THE THE THREE S'S--CHOW'S AT SEVEN.

I COULD USE ABOUT A GALLON OF COFFEE.

MR. JOURNAL, YOU STILL ALIVE?

BARELY.

IF YOU'LL COME WITH ME, SIR. THE OLD MAN WOULD LIKE TO APOLOGIZE FOR NOT GETTING TO YOU BEFORE. HE'S BUSIER THAN A TWO-DOLLAR WHORE ON SATURDAY NIGHT.

I UNDERSTAND.

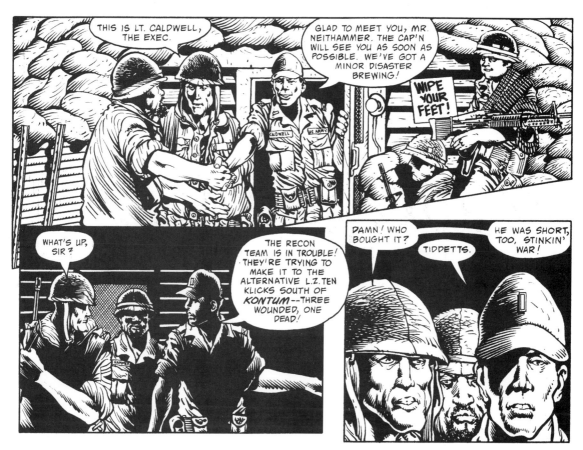

THIS IS LT. CALDWELL, THE EXEC.

GLAD TO MEET YOU, MR. NEITHAMMER. THE CAP'N WILL SEE YOU AS SOON AS POSSIBLE. WE'VE GOT A MINOR DISASTER BREWING!

WIPE YOUR FEET!

WHAT'S UP, SIR?

THE RECON TEAM IS IN TROUBLE! THEY'RE TRYING TO MAKE IT TO THE ALTERNATIVE L.Z. TEN KLICKS SOUTH OF *KONTUM*--THREE WOUNDED, ONE DEAD!

DAMN! WHO BOUGHT IT?

TIDDETTS.

HE WAS SHORT, TOO, STINKIN' WAR!

YOU THE REPORTER BATTALION BRIEFED ME ON? CAPT. SOLINSKI AT YOUR SERVICE, SIR.

MY PLEASURE.

I GOT THE FIRST CAV, ON THE HORN, CAPTAIN, THEY SAY THEY CAN SPARE TWO GUNSHIPS IN 30 --THREE-ZERO-- MINUTES, SIR.

THANK GOD!

DO YOU THINK YOU'LL GET THEM OUT?

SIR, I CAN HAVE MY SQUAD READY AND WAITING AT THE PAD--

I SHOULD HAVE KNOWN YOU'D VOLUNTEER, SGT. TEED. VERY WELL. I DON'T THINK YOU NEED ANY ADVICE FROM ME. YOU'VE BEEN ON TOO MANY OF THESE.

YESSIR, THANK YOU, SIR.

SO, YOU THINK MAYBE SGT. TEED IS LOOKING FOR A MEDAL OR SOMETHING?

NO, IT'S NOTHING LIKE THAT. HE THINKS A SOLDIER'S JOB IS KEEPING THE PEACE, AND IF THAT TAKES KICKING A LITTLE ASS--

HATES VIOLENCE SO MUCH HE GETS DOWNRIGHT VIOLENT ABOUT IT?

SOMETHING LIKE THAT.

LISTEN, I'D LIKE TO TAG ALONG.

I'M NOT SURE WHO YOU ARE, OR WHAT KIND OF PULL YOU HAVE FROM THE HIGHER ECHELON, BUT I'VE BEEN TOLD IN NO UNCERTAIN TERMS TO GIVE YOU A FREE REIN. IT'S YOUR BUTT!

ORDERLY ROOM

LOOK, I DON'T WANT TO STEP ON ANYONE'S TOES AROUND HERE. I'M JUST LIKE YOU--DOING A JOB.

NO PROBLEM. YOU'LL GET FULL COOPERATION FROM MY PEOPLE, EVEN TO THE BODY BAG WE SHIP YOU HOME IN. JUST ONE THING--

WHAT IS IT? YOU GOT A COUPLE OF SENATORS OR GENERALS IN YOUR BACK POCKET?

I DON'T--BUT IT WOULD SEEM THAT THE PEOPLE I WORK FOR DO.

THAT IT DO--THAT IT DO.

WHUMP WHUMP WHUMP WHUMP

"THE RHYTHMIC THROB OF THE CHOPPERS ANNOUNCED THEIR ARRIVAL AT THE PAD. I DIDN'T HAVE ANY TIME FOR BREAKFAST, BUT NEITHER DID ANYONE ELSE."

"I WAS SECRETLY THANKFUL. SKIMMING THE TREETOPS ON A ROLLER COASTER RIDE INTO BATTLE WITH A LOAD OF S.O.S. ON MY STOMACH --WELL, IT PROBABLY WOULDN'T HAVE STAYED DOWN ANYWAY."

WHUMP WHUMP

WHUMP WHUMP

"THE LOADING WAS UNEVENTFUL, UNLIKE THE DAY BEFORE WHEN I HAD ARRIVED. MAYBE THE SNIPER WAS SLEEPING IN."

"AND IN ONLY MOMENTS, WE LIFTED OFF NORTHWEST TOWARD KONTUM."

WHUMP WHUMP WHUMP WHUMP WHUMP WHUMP

YOU BETTER SIT ON YOUR HELMET, OLD TIMER--UNLESS YOU'VE GIVEN UP HOPE OF FATHER-ING KIDS ANY TIME IN THE FUTURE.

"EVERYONE HANDLES TENSION IN HIS OWN WAY--MALONE, THE DOOR GUNNER, TRIED TO TALK IT AWAY."

YEAH, I WAS T.D.Y. TO THE 199 TH BRAVO COM-PANY, IN THE DELTA. WE HAD A GROOVY LITTLE TECHNIQUE FOR FLUSHING CHARLIE--

AS SOON AS THE DOGS SNIFFED OUT THE TUNNELS, WE BROUGHT IN THE WATER CANNON AND *WHOOSH!* THE ONES WHO WEREN'T DROWNED IMMEDIATELY WERE BLOWN OUT LIKE JONAH THROUGH THE BLOWHOLE!

THEN SOME REPORTER GOT WIND OF IT AND PUT IT ON THE WIRES.

STIRRED UP A BUNCH OF CRAP AND PUBLIC OPINION FREAKED. DROWNING POOR CHARLIE IN HIS OWN STINKING TUNNELS WAS CRUEL AND UNUSUAL PUNISHMENT, SAYS THEY.

THE PENTAGON SENDS DOWN A DIRECTIVE: NO MORE USE OF THE WATER CANNON TO FLOOD THE TUNNELS...

WHUMP WHUMP WHUMP WHUMP

SO, WE FILLED THE TUNNELS WITH GASOLINE INSTEAD --WATER WAS CRUEL, BUT GASOLINE WAS ACCEPTABLE. DAMN STRANGE WAR.

AS SOON AS WE TOUCH DOWN, THE SQUAD FANS OUT TO LAY COVER FIRE WHILE THE RECON TEAM LOADS INTO THAT OTHER CHOPPER. IN AND OUT, QUICK AND SIMPLE.

FOXFIRE, THIS IS KEYSTONE. WE ROGER YOUR GREEN SMOKE.

SGT. TEED, YOUR PEOPLE MADE THE L.Z., THEY'RE UNDER FIRE AND IN A BAD WAY.

HOLD ON, HOLD ON.

"THE METAL SHELL OF THE HUEY GROANED FROM THE CENTRIFUGAL FORCE AS THE BODY OF THE SHIP ATTEMPTED TO MATCH THE MAIN ROTOR SPEED."

"SOMEHOW I CLUNG TO A VERTICAL STRUT. OTHERS WEREN'T SO FORTUNATE!"

AAAAAH!

JUDAS! WE'RE GOING INTO THE TREES!

COME ON, PEOPLE, THIS OLD GIRL HAS WHEEZED HER LAST.

LET'S GO, JOURNAL. THIS THING'S A BOMB JUST WAITING TO GO OFF!

YEAH-- RIGHT BEHIND YOU!

"I REMEMBER VERY LITTLE OF THE CRASH. PANIC--A BONE-JARRING BUMP-- AND A BLUR OF EMOTION!"

ALL RIGHT, LISTEN UP. THE OTHER CHOPPER SAW US GO DOWN. WE HAVE TO HOLD ON UNTIL THEY COME BACK TO GET US.

CHARLIE SAW US GO DOWN, TOO. IT'S ONLY A MATTER OF TIME UNTIL THEY'RE ON US LIKE STINK ON STYLES.

WHAT'S OUR CHANCE OF WALKING OUT?

SLIM. THIS IS AN AREA OF HEAVY, AND I MEAN *HEAVY* ENEMY ACTIVITY. OUR BEST CHANCE IS TO HUG THE L.Z. UNTIL WE'RE RESCUED.

WHERE YOU GOIN', JOURNAL?

GOTTA SEE A MAN ABOUT A DOG. I'LL BE BACK IN A MINUTE OR TWO.

"MODESTY IS A LUXURY BEST FOREGONE IN THE BOONDOCKS--"

DON'T WANDER TOO FAR. IT'S TOO EASY TO LOSE YOURSELF IN JUNGLE THIS THICK.

RIGHT, I'VE ALWAYS HAD A GOOD SENSE OF DIRECTION. I'LL BE FINE.

"I DROPPED DOWN INTO A GULLY ONLY YARDS FROM TEED'S SQUAD."

"LEAVE IT TO NATURE TO CALL AT THE MOST INOPPORTUNE TIME."

"BUT WHEN I ATTEMPTED TO RETURN TO THE DOWNED HELICOPTER--"

WHA-- SOMEONE COMING!

"VIET CONG! I HAD WONDERED WHAT I WOULD FEEL AT MY FIRST CONTACT WITH THEM."

"I DECIDED TO FOLLOW, HOPING THEY WERE HEADED TOWARD TEED'S SQUAD."

"NOW I KNEW-- COLD FEAR!"

"THEN AGAIN, FOR ALL I KNEW THEY WERE ON THEIR WAY TO HANOI FOR R&R!"

SPREAD OUT. SET UP A PERIMETER AT TEN METER INTERVALS. CORRE- LATE YOUR KILL-ZONES, AND DIG IN IF THERE'S TIME!

WHERE THE HELL IS HE? DAMN FOOL CIVILIAN!

YOU WANT ME TO TAKE A LOOK?

NO TIME. IF THE VC WANT HIM, THEY CAN HAVE HIM.

DAMN FOOL.

"SUDDENLY, THE WAR SEEMED FAR AWAY."

"BUT ONLY FOR A MOMENT!"

MY GOD! THEY DON'T HAVE A CHANCE!

"THERE WAS NOTHING I COULD DO AGAINST HALF A DOZEN ARMED CONG-- I HAD HEARD THE STORIES... "

"BUT--"

"THE REST OF THE SQUAD LAUGHED GOODNATUREDLY AS THE GIRLS SEVERELY THRASHED THEIR COMRADE..."

"...ONLY HELPING HIM OUT AFTER HE HAD NEARLY DROWNED!"

"I RETREATED BACK DOWN THE PATH THE WAY I HAD COME."

HOW STUPID. OF COURSE THERE ARE FEMALE *VC*. GUESS I NEVER THOUGHT ABOUT IT BEFORE.

"I REASONED THAT IF THE *VC* CAMP WAS AT ONE END OF THE PATH, THE GOOD GUYS OUGHT TO BE AT THE OTHER."

"I DIDN'T REALIZE UNTIL LATER HOW LUCKY I WAS THAT DAY. I NEVER TRIPPED A SINGLE BOOBY TRAP! I WAS MORE WORRIED ABOUT BEING EATEN ALIVE BY MOSQUITOES OR BOILED IN MY OWN SWEAT."

"THERE WAS NOTHING TO DO EXCEPT KEEP PUSHING FORWARD, HOUR BY HOUR. BUT THE PROSPECT OF SPENDING THE NIGHT ALONE IN THE JUNGLE FILLED ME WITH DREAD."

"FINALLY, AS I ROUNDED A CURVE--"

THANK GOD!

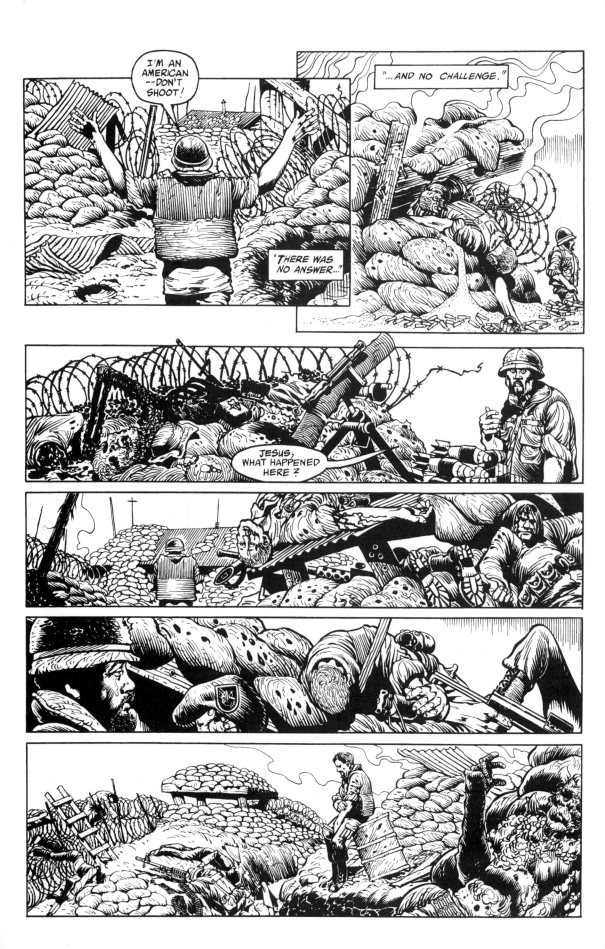

"I SAT THERE, MY MIND BLANK, UNTIL THE SUN WAS ONLY A FAINT GLOW."

"FINALLY, I COLLECTED MY THOUGHTS. I NEEDED FOOD."

"I FOUND SOME."

C RATION

C RATION

C RATION

WHA--WHO'S THERE?

NOBODY, MAN--

JUST US CORPSES.

IS--AH--IS THERE ANYTHING I CAN DO?

US ARMY

NO, MAN, THERE'S NOTHING ANYBODY CAN DO.

WHAT CAN I DO? MAYBE THERE'S STILL A RADIO WORKING.

NOT A CHANCE. DAMN LUNATIC SMASHED 'EM ALL BEFORE A SAPPER GOT HIM.

LOOK, I'LL SIT WITH YOU AS LONG AS YOU WANT. THERE'S A LOT OF EQUIPMENT LEFT HERE. THEY'LL BE BACK.

YEAH, YOU BETTER GET OUTTA HERE, MAN. DON'T WORRY ABOUT ME, I GOT IT FIGURED.

TELL ME ABOUT THE DOG.

OL' FRITZ? HE WAS A HELL OF A DOG. YOU KNOW, I NEVER HAD A PET WHEN I WAS A KID. NO EXPERIENCE WITH ANIMALS AT ALL. SO OF COURSE THE ARMY MADE ME A HANDLER. TYPICAL.

YOU KNOW, THEY TAUGHT US THAT COMBAT DOGS ARE TWENTY TIMES MORE AWARE THAN THE BEST SOLDIER. AND THAT SHEPHERDS ARE THE BEST FOR SIZE, ENDURANCE, STRENGTH, AND SMARTS. I'D RATHER HAVE FRITZ THAN A PLATOON OF REGULAR TROOPS.

BACK IN DECEMBER, AT *TAN SON NHUT* AIR BASE, A DOG NAMED KING ALERTED THE BASE TO A *VC* ATTACK. THEY LOST THREE GUARDS AND THREE DOGS BEFORE THE BASE WAS SECURE. 28 *VC* WERE KILLED AND FOUR WERE TAKEN PRISONER!

ONE OF THE DOGS TOOK A BULLET AND STILL KILLED TWO *VC*, SAVING HIS HANDLER'S ASS! LOYALTY LIKE THAT DON'T COME ALONG EVERY DAY!

LOOK, MAYBE I CAN RIG SOMETHING TO DRAG YOU INTO THE JUNGLE. IF WE'RE LUCKY, THEY WON'T FIND US. MAYBE TOMORROW--

FORGET IT, MAN, SAVE YOURSELF. I GOT IT FIGURED.

"IT WAS OBVIOUS HE WAS IN SHOCK AND SLIPPING. IT WAS ALSO OBVIOUS HE DID NOT WANT TO FACE THE SITUATION."

I STARTED WORKING WITH FRITZ WHEN HE WAS FIFTEEN MONTHS OLD. HE WAS STUPID, BUT HE HAD THAT SOMETHING--YOU KNOW, HEART, A LOT OF HEART!

"HE WENT THROUGH OBEDIENCE TRAINING LIKE A BREEZE. HE WOULD SPEND A DAY ON THE OBSTACLE COURSE--AND WHEN I WAS DRAGGING MYSELF BACK TO THE BILLETS, HE WAS STILL FRESH AND WANTING MORE! GOD, HE USED TO WEAR ME OUT!"

"AND WHEN HE ATTACKED, HE ATTACKED WITH A VENGEANCE. HE RIPPED APART HIS SHARE OF ATTACK DUMMIES!'"

"'BUT THE BEST TIMES WERE THE OFF-DUTY TIMES. JUST BEING TOGETHER, A CHANCE FOR BOTH OF US TO FORGET THIS STINKING WAR!'"

"'MY ONLY COMPLAINT IS HE USED TO HOG THE BLANKET.'"

"THEY THREW EVERY DIRTY JOB IMAGINABLE AT US--
FROM DIGGING OUT *VC* TUNNELS--'"

"'-TO GOING IN AFTER THE BASTARDS.
FRITZ WAS FEARLESS.'"

"'TRUTH BE KNOWN, HE
SAVED A LOT OF ENEMY
LIVES. THEY WOULD
SURRENDER RATHER
THAN FACE THOSE
TEETH !'"

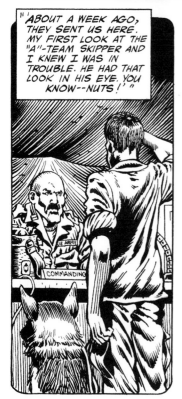

"'ABOUT A WEEK AGO,
THEY SENT US HERE.
MY FIRST LOOK AT THE
"A"-TEAM SKIPPER AND
I KNEW I WAS IN
TROUBLE. HE HAD THAT
LOOK IN HIS EYE. YOU
KNOW--NUTS !'"

"'WE KEPT TO OURSELVES
PRETTY MUCH. JUST DID
OUR JOB.'"

"'THEN, LAST EVENING, OUR *ARVN*
PATROL REPORTED A MAJOR
BUILDUP OF VIET CONG AND
NORTH VIETNAMESE REGULARS.'"

"'WE WERE SURROUNDED!'"

"THERE WAS NO MENTION OF IT IN THE DAILY REPORT. NO HINT OF THE IMMINENT ATTACK--"

BUT, SIR--

SEND IT. "NEGATIVE CONTACT."

"NOBODY COULD SLEEP, ESPECIALLY FRITZ. HE SENSED DANGER VERY CLOSE.'"

EASY, BOY. I KNOW. I KNOW.

"THE MORTAR BARRAGE STARTED ABOUT 0300."

"WE LOST OUR TWO 81'S SHORTLY AFTER THE SATURATION BEGAN--'"

"--AND WITH ONLY HALF A DOZEN M-79 GRENADE LAUNCHERS LEFT, OUR DEFENSE LOOKED BLEAK!"

CAP'N, YOU GOTTA CALL IT IN! WE NEED AIR SUPPORT!

SHUT UP AND GET BACK TO YOUR POSITION OR I'LL HAVE YOUR ASS UP ON CHARGES. THIS FIRE TEAM DOES NOT ADMIT FAILURE! WE STAND TO THE LAST MAN, SOLDIER, IS THAT UNDERSTOOD?

"AS I LEFT, HE WAS SINGING CADENCE, FOR GOD'S SAKE--CADENCE!

I WANT TO BE AN AIRBORNE RANGER, I WANT TO LIVE A LIFE OF DANGER...

I HELD HIM TILL HE DIED. HE HURT A LONG TIME.

A LONG TIME.

"I TRIED TO THINK OF A WAY TO GET HIM OUT OF THE COMPOUND EVEN THOUGH HE COULDN'T LAST THE NIGHT. I FELT I HAD TO TRY!"

"SUDDENLY--"

VIET CONG!

TROOPER! TROOPER! WE GOTTA GET OUTTA HERE ENEMY SOLDIERS!

THEY'RE EVERY-WHERE, MAN. THERE AIN'T NO PLACE TO HIDE.

SAVE YOURSELF, MAN, I GOT IT FIGURED.

"MY HEART WAS IN MY THROAT AS I WATCHED THEIR APPROACH."

CHA-CLICK!

"IT WAS NEARLY EVENING THE NEXT DAY..."

DOES THIS BELONG TO YOU, TEED?

MR. NEITHAMMER, THE 618TH TOLD US YOU WERE HITCHING A RIDE BACK WITH THEM.

GLAD TO SEE YOU. I WOULDN'T BLAME YOU IF YOU BROKE MY JAW FOR RUNNING OUT ON YOU.

DON'T WORRY ABOUT THAT, IT WAS MY OWN FAULT. YOU HAD NO CHOICE.

I JUST WANT TO GET A HOT MEAL AND ABOUT TEN HOURS OF SLEEP. THEN I'VE GOT AN ARTICLE TO WRITE FOR MY MAGAZINE.

SOMETHING ABOUT THE ROCKETS' RED GLARE AND BOMBS BURSTING IN AIR?

NO, SOMETHING ABOUT FRIENDSHIP.

THE FRIENDSHIP OF A DOG NAMED FRITZ AND A TROOPER --I NEVER KNEW HIS NAME.

FEBRUARY 19, 1967. DELTA CAMP 267. 0300 HOURS. THE CENTRAL HIGHLANDS, SOUTH VIETNAM.

YEAH, THIS IS A TWO-MAN GUARD POST. TWO HOURS ON DUTY, FOUR HOURS OFF.

HOW OFTEN DO YOU PULL GUARD?

'BOUT TWICE A WEEK-- 'LOT BETTER'N THE LAST PLACE I WAS AT.

HOW'S THAT?

I SPENT FOUR MONTHS *TDY* AT A GUARD COMPANY AT THE *QUI NOHN* AIRPORT. THAT WAS A BITCH. ALL THEY DID WAS GUARD ONE THING OR ANOTHER--WHAT A BUMMER.

LOOKS LIKE THAT GUITAR HAS SEEN A LOT OF ACTION.

THAT'S *FRIENDLY FIRE*--

A COUPLE OF WEEKS AGO TUCKER'S BUNK MATES, UNDERWHELMED WITH HIS PICKIN', TOOK IT AWAY FROM HIM.

THE WORLD'S FULL OF CRITICS.

THEY LEANED IT AGAINST A SAND-BAGGED BUNKER AND UNLOADED A FULL MAGAZINE FROM AN *M-16* INTO IT.

WHAT DID YOU DO?

AW, THEY DIDN'T DO ANY REAL HARM--JUST A COUPLE OF STRINGS. I REPLACED THEM AND IT SOUNDS FINE NOW.

IN FACT, I THINK IT IMPROVED THE TONE.

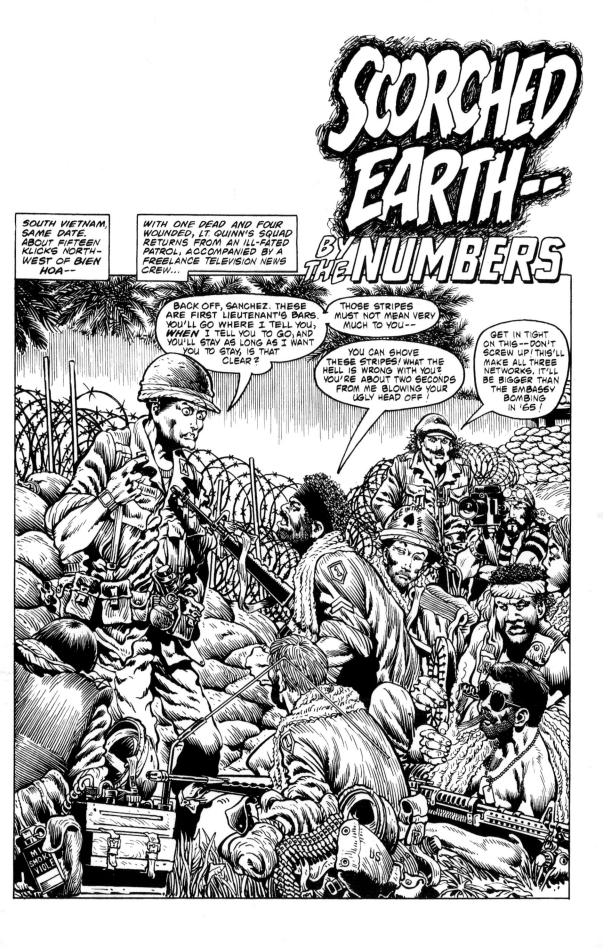

FEBRUARY 22, 1967. DELTA CAMP 267. 0816 HOURS.

A BIG FAT AFFIRMATIVE ON THAT, JOURNAL. THIS IS MY LAST WORK DAY IN BEAUTIFUL SOUTHEAST ASIA, PEARL OF THE GODDAMN ORIENT. TOMORROW IT'S *PLEIKU*, *CAM RANH BAY*, THEN THE *WORLD!*

CONGRATULATIONS.

I UNDERSTAND THAT TRASH RUN OF YOURS CAN BE PRETTY STICKY--THE DUMP IS WAY OUT IN THE BOONDOCKS, ISN'T IT?

YEAH, IT'S A FULL DAY'S DRIVE THERE AND BACK. AND THE ROAD AIN'T THAT SECURE-- IT CAN BE HAIRY!

MIND IF I TAG ALONG?

IF YOU DON'T MIND THREE IN THE CAB. THE POOR SOUL WHO'S PULLING THE DETAIL FROM NOW ON IS RIDING ALONG.

"WITH THE HELP OF THREE A.I.K. CIVILIAN LABORERS, THE TRUCK WAS LOADED IN ABOUT AN HOUR AND A HALF. WEBBER, THE YOUNG PRIVATE, SEEMED APPREHENSIVE."

DON'T WORRY, KID. YOU PAY CLOSE ATTENTION TO HOW I MAKE THIS RUN AND YOU'LL ROTATE BACK TO THE WORLD WITHOUT A SCRATCH. JUST LIKE YOURS TRULY.

TRUST ME, KID.

I'VE HEARD A LOT OF STORIES ABOUT THE AREA WE'LL BE GOING THROUGH. YOU DON'T EVEN HAVE YOUR FLACK JACKET AND HELMET ALONG!

"WE WERE ABOUT SEVEN KILOMETERS FROM THE MAIN GATE OF CAMP 267 WHEN--"

WHAT'S THE MATTER? WHERE ARE WE GOING?

"THE NARROW, RUTTED ROAD LED THROUGH A GROVE OF TREES AND INTO A SMALL HAMLET OF THATCHED SOD HOUSES."

"AFTER A SHORT CONVERSATION WITH AN ELDERLY VIETNAMESE, DANCER RETURNED TO THE TRUCK FOLLOWED BY A DOZEN OR SO VILLAGERS."

THEY'RE UNLOADING!

THAT'S RIGHT. THIS IS WHERE I COME EVERY WEEK INSTEAD OF RISKING MY LIFE ON ONE OF THE MOST DANGER- OUS STRETCHES OF ROAD IN THIS WHOLE DAMN COUNTRY!

THEY'RE REAL TICKLED TO GET IT. YOU KNOW THE GOVERN- MENT THROWS AWAY A LOT OF USEFUL STUFF. THEY UNLOAD IT --PAY ME FIVE BUCKS--I DON'T GET KILLED. HELL OF A DEAL.

DANCER US ARMY

AND THE WAITING AIN'T BAD, EITHER

US AR

MAJOR, THIS MAY BE AS CLOSE TO SUBSTANTIAL ENEMY FORCES AS WE'LL GET FOR A WHILE--

WHAT ARE YOU SUGGESTING?

THEY'RE ALREADY ON THE RUN. WITH THREE GUNSHIPS TO BACK YOU UP, WELL, ANYTHING WE PUT ON THE WIRE TODAY CAN BE SEEN BY THOSE ARM-CHAIR QUARTERBACKS IN THE PENTAGON ON THE SIX O'CLOCK NEWS TOMORROW NIGHT. IT CAN'T DO YOUR CAREER ANY HARM.

YES, I SEE WHAT YOU MEAN.

SIR! ONE OF THOSE HUEYS IS FULL OF *MY BLEEDING TROOPS.*

THEN YOU AND YOUR PEOPLE HAD BETTER GET MOVING. I WANT THOSE *VC* BODIES ACCOUNTED FOR. THIS WAY, MR. FEINSTEIN. I'LL SHOW THOSE FAT-ASSED BUREAUCRATS HOW WE TAKE CHARGE!

WE'RE NOT MOVING ONE STEP UNTIL THAT CHOPPER IS AIRBORNE!

ARE YOU REFUSING A DIRECT ORDER, SERGEANT?

WHY NOT ACCOMODATE HIM, MAJOR? WE'RE LOSING THE LIGHT!

YES, OF COURSE, SERGEANT, EVAC THE WOUNDED *ASAP.* THEY'RE ALWAYS MY PRIORITY!

RIGHT, GET THAT CHOPPER AIRBORNE --MOVE IT!

BUT WHEN THE BODIES ARE DRAGGED FROM THE UNDERGROWTH, T.D. FEINSTEIN, NETWORK CORRESPONDENT, IS DISAPPOINTED.

THAT'S ALL? TWO BODIES?

HMMM-- IF THERE WERE MORE THEY WERE DRAGGED INTO THE TUNNELS BY THEIR COMRADES.

TUNNELS?

YES, THIS ENTIRE AREA FROM HERE TO THE RIVER IS HONEYCOMBED WITH MILES OF *VIET CONG* TUNNELS.

OVER HERE, SIR. THEY DIDN'T HAVE TIME TO CLOSE THE *"DOOR"* BEHIND THEM.

SIR? WARRANT OFFICER VAN METER IS GETTING ANTSY. HE SAYS THAT THOSE GUNSHIPS ARE SITTING DUCKS IN THAT CLEARING--

I SWEAR THAT MAN IS AFRAID OF HIS OWN SHADOW.

MAYBE THE FACT THAT HE'S BEEN SHOT DOWN *TWICE* MAKES HIM A LITTLE JUMPY.

TELL HIM TO MAKE A WIDE CIRCLE AND CHECK WITH OUR RADIO MAN EVERY TEN MINUTES. WE NEED TIME TO FLUSH 'EM OUT.

YOU CAN'T MEAN THAT, SIR.

DON'T WORRY, SERGEANT. I BROUGHT A SQUAD OF TUNNEL RATS FROM BATALLION. THEY'VE DRAGGED CHARLIE--KICKING AND SCREAMING--FROM HIS HOLE BEFORE. CORPORAL PYEATT, FRONT AND CENTER.

WHUMP WHUMP WHUMP WHUMP

CORPORAL PYEATT REPORTING, SIR!

GO GET 'EM, SON. WE STILL HAVE A CHANCE TO TURN THIS SORRY PERFORMANCE INTO A SUCCESSFUL MISSION.

I DON'T KNOW, SIR. IT'S BEEN TOO LONG. THEY'VE HAD PLENTY OF TIME TO SET UP TRAPS AND WIRES.

YOU'LL BE FINE, SOLDIER.

THIS IS STUPID. THIS WHOLE DAMN SHOW IS FOR THE CAMERA. YOU'RE ALL ACTING LIKE A BUNCH OF RAW RECRUITS.

ONE GRENADE COULD KILL YOU ALL-- SPREAD OUT AND STAY AWAKE.

HOW'S THE LIGHT?

NOT GOOD. WE'VE GOT LESS THAN HALF AN HOUR.

I DON'T LIKE THIS, SWEAR TO GOD I DON'T!

GOING IN THERE WITHOUT DOGS IS SUICIDE!

ALL RIGHT, LET'S DO THE SPOT NOW, WE CAN ADD A TAG LATER IF ANYTHING COMES OF THIS.

RIGHT.

MAJOR--OVER HERE. I WANT TO FILM AN INTERVIEW WITH YOU.

YES, OF COURSE!

WE'RE HERE WITH THE 199TH INFANTRY BRIGADE, NEAR *VINH LONG* IN THE *MEKONG DELTA*, AS A LIFE AND DEATH DRAMA UNFOLDS BEFORE OUR VERY EYES. MAJOR SEATON, COULD YOU EXPLAIN WHAT IS GOING ON HERE?

WHIRRR

AH...YES, THIS IS A TYPICAL *VIET CONG* TUNNEL COMPLEX THAT THE ENEMY USES TO CONDUCT HIS COMINGS AND GOINGS. EVEN AFTER ONE OF THESE SYSTEMS IS DISCOVERED, THERE IS NO EASY WAY OF ROOTING OUT THE COMMUNISTS. ARTILLERY HAS NO EFFECT.

WHIRR

YES, IN THIS MODERN AGE OF MECHANIZED WARFARE THE REALLY DIRTY JOBS, AS IN WARS PAST, ARE LEFT TO THE FOOT SOLDIER, THE UNGLAMOROUS JOB OF FACING THE UNKNOWN DANGERS OF THOSE DARK TUNNELS AND CONFRONTING "CHARLIE" ON HIS OWN TERMS FALLS TO THESE SOLDIERS.

WHIRRRR

TELL ME, PRIVATE, HOW DO YOU FEEL ABOUT--

I'LL TELL YOU HOW I FEEL. THIS SUCKS. THIS WHOLE ROTTEN SITUATION SUCKS.

WHHIRRR

ALL RIGHT, CUT-- WE'LL REWORK THIS LATER. RIGHT NOW, JUST FILM THE ACTION WITHOUT SOUND. I'LL MATCH A TRACK TO IT IF IT COMES TO ANYTHING.

WHIRR

SIR, VAN METER IS ON THE RADIO. HE SAYS THEY ONLY HAVE ABOUT 20 MINUTES OF FUEL LEFT.

TELL HIM I'LL GET BACK TO HIM.

ONE OF THEM IS COMING OUT!

THERE'RE BODIES IN THERE, SIR. IT LOOKS LIKE THEY DRUG THEM IN THERE A SHORT DISTANCE AND LEFT THEM.

HOW MANY?

FIVE, MAYBE SIX. CAN'T TELL FOR SURE-- SOME OF THEM ARE IN PIECES!

IT LOOKS LIKE YOUR PEOPLE DID BETTER THAN YOU THOUGHT, SERGEANT TRAPP!

HAVE THEM DRAG THE STIFFS OUT HERE. YOU'D LOOK GREAT STANDING OVER SEVEN OR EIGHT DEAD V.C. YOU MIGHT EVEN GET YOUR PICTURE IN THE STARS AND STRIPES.

HOW ABOUT TRIPWIRES OR BOOBYTRAPS?

NOTHING, SIR. THE TUNNEL'S CLEAN CLEAR BACK TO WHERE THEY STACKED THE BODIES.

TELL THE OTHERS TO START DRAGGING THEM OUT. I WANT A CONFIRMED BODY COUNT.

YESSIR!

FEBRUARY 28, 1967. DELTA CAMP 267, 2127 HOURS.

WEBBER? MY GOD, ARE YOU ALL RIGHT? YOU LOOK TERRIBLE.

JUST TAG AND BAG ME, MAN. I SWEAR TO GOD I'LL NEVER MAKE IT THROUGH ANOTHER DAY LIKE THIS ONE.

YOU MEAN YOU'RE JUST GETTING BACK FROM THE TRASH RUN?

YEAH, AND I'M DAMN LUCKY TO BE ALIVE! WHAT A NIGHTMARE!

YOU DIDN'T TAKE DANCER'S ADVICE?

HOW'D YOU GUESS?

THE TRIP WAS A DISASTER FROM THE START. BUT I GOT INTEGRITY, MAN. I FIGURED IF I WAS GOING TO DO THE JOB, I WAS GOING TO DO IT THE WAY IT WAS SUPPOSED TO BE DONE.

"IT WAS LATE WHEN WE FINALLY GOT THE TRUCK LOADED. WE ABOUT BROKE OUR BACKS LOADING A BUNCH OF 55 GALLON DRUMS HALF FULL OF SOME STICKY, FOUL-SMELLING STUFF--PROBABLY TOXIC. THE ROAD WAS EVEN WORSE THAN I HAD HEARD!"

RUDDD
RUDDD
RUDD

"ABOUT HALF-WAY, I GOT A FLAT--ON AN INSIDE DUAL, OF COURSE."

"I HAD THE TIRE ABOUT HALF-CHANGED WHEN A DEUCE-AND-A-HALF FROM ANOTHER COMPANY CAME AROUND THE CORNER."

BEEP BEEP

"MY RIG WAS BLOCKING THE ROAD. THE DRIVER GOT DOWN AND CAME TOWARD ME, PROBABLY TO GIVE ME A PIECE OF HIS MIND--"

"IT WAS LIKE SLOW-MOTION--MOVEMENT IN THE TREES, A TRAIL OF SMOKE--AND THE OTHER TRUCK EXPLODED!"

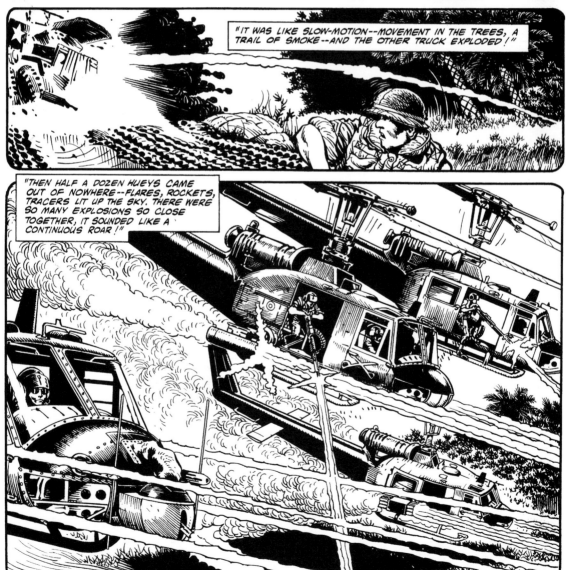

"THEN HALF A DOZEN HUEYS CAME OUT OF NOWHERE--FLARES, ROCKETS, TRACERS LIT UP THE SKY. THERE WERE SO MANY EXPLOSIONS SO CLOSE TOGETHER, IT SOUNDED LIKE A CONTINUOUS ROAR!"

IT WAS QUITE A SHOW. FINALLY THINGS CLEARED UP ENOUGH FOR US TO FINISH AND GET OUT OF THERE. SINCE WE COULDN'T PASS THE BURNING TRUCK, WE TURNED AROUND AND CAME BACK.

I DROPPED THE OTHER DRIVER AT HIS COMPANY, AND HERE I AM. I STILL GOT TO GET RID OF THAT LOAD TOMORROW.

BACK TO THE DUMP?

TO HELL WITH INTEGRITY! I'LL TAKE DANCER'S ROUTE TOMORROW AND MAKE A QUICK FIVE BUCKS.

HEY, JOURNAL! HOW'S IT GOING?

TEED, COME ON IN HERE. WHAT'S NEW?

I JUST CAME FROM A MEETING WITH THE BRASS. DID YOU KNOW A TV NEWS CREW JUST ARRIVED?

REALLY? WHICH NETWORK?

I DON'T KNOW. THE MAN IN CHARGE IS ONE T.D. FEINSTEIN. YOU KNOW HIM?

WE'VE MET. IN '64 AT THE *KAMINA BASE* IN *KATANGA*, AFRICA. HE HAS A REAL TECHNIQUE FOR NOSING OUT THE HOT SPOTS.

HE WAS A MASTER AT TURNING MOLEHILLS INTO MOUNTAINS. I'D KEEP AN EYE ON HIM, SARGE.

MARCH 9, 1967.
1521 HOURS.

IT HAD BEEN ONE OF THOSE ENDLESS, POINTLESS MISSIONS NEAR THE *CAMBODIAN BORDER.* WE'D BEEN OUT FOR DAYS IN THE RAIN AND THE STINK.

THE TENSION WAS RELENTLESS. EACH OF US KNEW THAT AT ANY MOMENT A SNIPER'S BULLET COULD TURN OUR BRAINS INTO A CLOUD OF PINK HAZE.

NO ENEMY CONTACT AND I'VE GOT A DEADLINE. HOW LONG DO THESE PATROLS USUALLY LAST?

A WEEK, SOMETIMES TWO. THAT'S WHY THEY CALL THEM *LARPS* -- LONG RANGE RECON PATROLS.

IT WAS OBVIOUS MR. T.D. FEINSTEIN WAS FRUSTRATED. THREE DAYS AND THEY HADN'T EXPOSED MORE THAN A YARD OF FILM.

I KNOW WHAT IT MEANS. I'VE SEEN MORE ACTION THAN ALL OF THESE KIDS PUT TOGETHER! AFRICA, CHILE, CENTRAL AMERICA--

UH-HUH --OL' ANYTHING-FOR-A-STORY FEINSTEIN. YEAH, I REMEMBER YOU.

YOU DON'T THINK MUCH OF ME, DO YOU? WELL, IT DOESN'T MATTER. I'M NOT HERE TO MAKE FRIENDS. I'M *THAT FAR* FROM A NETWORK CORRESPONDENT ASSIGNMENT.

I'LL HAVE CRONKITE'S JOB BEFORE I'M THROUGH!

YOU'RE A DINOSAUR, OLD MAN. THIS IS THE WAVE OF THE FUTURE. ELECTRONIC MEDIA, NOT THAT WEEKLY NEWS MAGAZINE YOU WRITE FOR-- *THE GERITOL CROWD.* YOU GOTTA SEND PROOF OF SENILITY BEFORE THEY HONOR YOUR SUBSCRIPTION!

BY THE TIME WE CAME TO THE HAMLET, NERVES WERE AT THE BREAKING POINT. LACK OF SLEEP HAD LEFT US ALL PARANOID.

GET OVER THERE, DINK! YOU *VC*, HUH? YOU *VC*, BITCH?

INTELLIGENCE HAD REPORTED HEAVY ENEMY PRESENCE IN THE AREA. BUT A HOOTCH TO HOOTCH SEARCH TURNED UP NO *VC* OR WEAPONS.

THEY'RE LYING, SARGE, YOU KNOW THAT. THEY'RE ALL *VC!*

CALM DOWN, WE'RE NOT VIGILANTES!

NOW WHAT'S FEINSTEIN UP TO?

MOMENTS LATER --

FIRE!

YEAH, BURN THEM DOWN!

ALL RIGHT, YOU PEOPLE, *KNOCK IT OFF!* STYLES! ANDERSON! FALL IN OVER HERE!

NOW!!

I COULDN'T GET THE INCIDENT OUT OF MY MIND. IF IT WERE NOT FOR THE STRONG LEADERSHIP OF SGT. TEED, REPERCUSSIONS MIGHT HAVE BEEN FELT AROUND THE WORLD.

BURREL, I'M GOING TO NEED THE PHONE FOR QUITE A WHILE. CAN YOU SET IT UP FOR ME?

SURE, MR. NEITHAMMER. GOT A HOT STORY TO GET OUT?

NO, TRYING MY DAMEDNEST TO KEEP ANY MORE FROM DEVELOPING.

YEAH, WELL, THERE'S COFFEE IN THE POT AND I'LL BE IN THE AREA IF YOU NEED ANY HELP.

MUCH LATER --

ARE YOU STILL AT IT?

YEAH, I THINK MY EAR IS GOING TO FALL OFF. I'VE FOUND OUT SOME VERY DISTURBING THINGS ABOUT OUR MR. T.D. FEINSTEIN.

BEFORE COMING HERE, HE MADE A BRIEF STOP AT THE 199TH IN THE DELTA--DISASTER! BEFORE THAT, THE 4TH INFANTRY --THE 101ST AIRBORNE--THE 11TH AVIATION --AND THE BIG RED ONE.

BUSY. I SAW YOU MISSED SUPPER--I HAD THE COOK SAVE SOME FOR YOU.

THANKS. EVERY STOP HE'S MANIPULATED THE NEWS, AND TO HELL WITH ANYONE WHO GOT HURT!

SO I GOT IN TOUCH WITH GENERAL WESTMORELAND'S OFFICE. THEY'VE NEVER HEARD OF HIM!

AS FAR AS THEY KNOW, HE HAS NO AUTHORIZATION TO BE HERE --FROM OUR SIDE OR THE VIETNAMESE GOVERNMENT. IT SEEMS HE STOWED AWAY ON A C-130 FROM THE PHILIPPINES AND HAS BEEN MAKING OUT ON BRASS AND BULL SINCE.

LATER THAT NIGHT...

MR. JOURNAL, YOUR RIDE'S HERE.

YEAH, RIGHT. BE RIGHT THERE.

WHEN I GOT TO THE PAD THERE SEEMED TO BE A LARGER-THAN-USUAL CROWD OF ONLOOKERS.

WHAT THE HELL IS HE DOING HERE?

I INSISTED -- I THOUGHT MR. FEINSTEIN WOULD HAVE AN EXTREME INTEREST IN YOUR TRIP.

WHY SHOULD I GIVE A DAMN WHAT GRANDPA DOES?

YOU SHOWED A HELL OF A LOT OF INTEREST IN THIS BIRD LAST NIGHT --

I DON'T KNOW WHAT YOU'RE TALKING ABOUT --

THEN YOU WON'T MIND RIDING ALONG?

WHAT -- WHAT DO YOU MEAN?

I MEAN IT IS A BEAUTIFUL DAY FOR A RIDE IN A HELICOPTER, DON'T YOU THINK?

NO, WAIT -- I'M NOT GOING ANYWHERE!

LISTEN TO ME--YOU CAN'T DO THIS! YOU *CAN'T!!*

FEINSTEIN'S "AMBITION" HAD NEARLY COST ME MY LIFE AND *HAD* COST THE LIVES OF SEVERAL OTHERS. STILL I DID NOT LIKE THE DRAMA I SAW PLAYING OUT BEFORE ME.

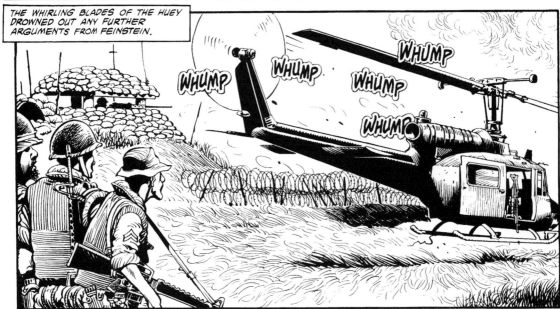

THE WHIRLING BLADES OF THE HUEY DROWNED OUT ANY FURTHER ARGUMENTS FROM FEINSTEIN.

WHUMP
WHUMP
WHUMP
WHUMP
WHUMP

FACING DEATH IN WARTIME WAS PART OF A SOLDIER'S JOB. DYING FOR A JUICY 15-SECOND SPOT ON THE TV NEWS WASN'T.

LATER REPORTS SAID THAT T.D. FEINSTEIN HAD BEEN FLOWN HOME AFTER AN ACCIDENT THAT LEFT HIM WITH TWO FRACTURED LEGS. DETAILS WERE SKETCHY. A REGIONAL PRESS ASSOCIATION GAVE HIM AN AWARD FOR RISKING LIFE AND LIMB TO GET THE STORY.

BIRDS OF PREY

SUNDAY, MARCH 12, 1967. 0921 HOURS. AN KHE, SOUTH VIETNAM.

OPERATION JUNCTION CITY, THE LARGEST TO DATE, WAS IN FULL SWING IN WAR ZONE C, NORTHWEST OF SAIGON. SSGT. TEED'S COMPANY HAD JUST RECEIVED ORDERS TO PREPARE TO MOVE OPERATIONS TO III CORPS AND LINK UP WITH THE 196 LIGHT INFANTRY BRIGADE AND THE 11TH ARMORED CAVALRY IN TAY NINH PROVINCE.

DELTA CAMP 267, NOW SECURE AND FULLY OPERATIONAL, WOULD BE TURNED OVER TO THE ARMY OF THE REPUBLIC OF VIETNAM TO CONDUCT OPERATIONS AGAINST INFILTRATION OF MEN AND MATERIEL INTO II CORPS VIA THE HO CHI MINH TRAIL IN CAMBODIA.

GOOD LUCK, JOURNAL. NOW REMEMBER, IF YOU WANT TO MOVE SOUTH WITH US, YOU HAVE YOUR JOURNALISTIC BUTT STANDING TALL AT THE PLEIKU AIRPORT WEDNESDAY A.M.

I'LL BE THERE, IF I DON'T GET LOST.

YOU DO MAKE A HABIT OF THAT, DON'T YOU?

I DON'T ALLOW NO MIDDLE-AGED GRUNTS TRACKING MUD ALL OVER MY NICE CLEAN LANDING PAD.

ONLY REASON YOU GOT A LANDING PAD IS BECAUSE NO OTHER FLIGHT CREW WOULD LET THAT SORRY TUB OF DUNG YOU FLY SET NEXT TO THEM AND STINK UP THE AREA!

HEY! YOU CAN TRASH MY WIFE AND KICK MY DOG, BUT DON'T YOU MEAN-MOUTH *SUGAR*, YOU BUTT WAD!

SON OF A BITCH!

HEY, THAT'S "SON OF A BITCH, SIR!"

SORRY, SON OF A BITCH, *SIR*!

TEED, HOW YA BEEN? I HAVEN'T SEEN YOU SINCE THE BOB HOPE CHRISTMAS SHOW.

YOU DIDN'T SEE MUCH OF ME THEN, EITHER. YOU DIDN'T SEE MUCH OF ANYTHING, AS I RECALL.

YES, I WAS A TAD WASTED THAT PARTICULAR DAY.

THAT PARTICULAR *WEEK*!

WELL, I *DO* HAVE A REPUTATION TO MAINTAIN.

WHAT HAVE WE HERE?

THIS IS SCOTT NEITHAMMER.

CALL ME JOURNAL.

JOURNAL, MEET ONE "MOONSHINE" McCOY, ASPIRING HILLBILLY SINGER, HELICOPTER PILOT, AND BORDERLINE PSYCHOTIC.

YOU LEFT OUT PRACTICING ALCOHOLIC. GLAD TO MEET YOU, JOURNAL.

THE CO-PILOT IS WARRANT OFFICER ANTHONY DaROSA. THAT LITTLE STROLL AROUND THE AIRCRAFT ISN'T JUST FOR EXERCISE. THERE ARE SOME 63 CHECKS TO MAKE BEFORE THEY EVEN CLIMB INSIDE.

Sweet SUGAR

SEE, A HUEY AIN'T A "KICK THE TIRES, LIGHT THE FIRES, AND GO" TYPE OF AIRCRAFT. GUESS THAT'S WHY SO MANY CHOPPER PILOTS ARE SUCH PAINS IN THE ASS.

AIRPLANES ARE LIGHT, AIRY, AND LOVE TO FLY. ENGINE QUITS? NO PROBLEM. GLIDE A WHILE ON THE AIR CURRENTS UNTIL YOU FIGURE OUT WHAT YOU'RE GONNA DO WITH HER.

ON THE OTHER HAND, A CHOPPER VIOLATES EVERY GODDAMN LAW OF NATURE! ENGINE QUITS, YOU DROP LIKE A STONE.

THAT'S COMFORTING.

THE CO-PILOT CIRCLED THE AIRCRAFT PUSHING, PULLING, TWISTING, TURNING, OPENING, CLOSING, AND PEEKING.

HE'S FINISHING UP NOW, CHECKING THE ROTOR HUB AND THE "JESUS NUT".

THE WHAT?

THE "JESUS NUT". IF IT COMES OFF, YOU GET TO MEET JESUS!

HMMM.

WHAT ARE YOU CARRYING?

RIGHT HERE IS A NOSE-MOUNTED M-5 40mm GRENADE LAUNCHER. IT CAN FIRE 107 ROUNDS QUICKER THAN A BAR GIRL DOWNS *SAIGON TEA.* YOU CAN DO YOUR SPRING PLOW-ING IN NO TIME WITH THIS.

ON EITHER SIDE, THERE ARE TWO 2.75-INCH SEVEN-TUBE ROCKET PODS.

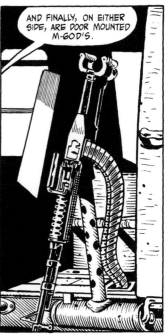

AND FINALLY, ON EITHER SIDE, ARE DOOR MOUNTED M-60D'S.

I SEE SOME DIFFERENCES BETWEEN THIS GUNSHIP AND THOSE OTHER HUEYS.

YEAH, THOSE ARE UH-1 "DELTAS." THEY'VE GOT LONGER FUSELAGES. WE CALL 'EM "SLICKS" 'CAUSE THEIR WEAPONRY IS MINIMAL. USE 'EM MAINLY FOR TROOP TRANSPORT.

BUFFALO BOB

THEY CARRY 14 WHILE THESE "BRAVO" MODELS ARE RECOMMENDED TO CARRY NINE.

RECOMMENDED?

WELL, HELL, WHEN YOU'RE PULLING TROOPS OUT OF A HOT *LZ,* THINGS CAN GET DESPERATE. YOU PILE ON AS MANY AS CAN GET A HANDHOLD.

UNDERSTOOD.

US ARMY

WE HEADED WEST AT A COMFORTABLE ALTITUDE. THE LUSH GREEN MOUNTAINS WERE ACCENTED BY OCCASIONAL SILVER LAKES AND STREAMS. FROM UP THERE, AT LEAST, VIETNAM WAS BEAUTIFUL COUNTRY.

WHUMP
WHUMP WHUMP
WHUMP

IT'S GONNA BE A LONG FLIGHT, SO YOU MIGHT AS WELL SETTLE BACK, JOURNAL.

WHAT'S THIS MISSION ABOUT?

HAVE YOU EVER HEARD OF THE CIDG, THE CIVILIAN IRREGULAR DEFENSE GROUP?

KIND OF A NATIONAL GUARD?

YEAH, PRETTY CLOSE. THE CIA TRAINS VARIOUS HILL TRIBES TO PROTECT THEIR OWN VILLAGES AGAINST THE VC. THE IDEA IS TO THROW A MONKEY WRENCH INTO NORTH VIETNAMESE INFILTRATION INTO REMOTE AREAS ALONG THE LAOS AND CAMBODIAN BORDERS.

IT'S A NATURAL, SINCE THE 'YARDS DON'T LIKE OR TRUST VIETNAMESE IN GENERAL, NORTH OR SOUTH.

THE BIGGEST PROBLEM WAS TO POINT THEM AT MORE NORTH VIETNAMESE THAN SOUTH VIETNAMESE. IT DOESN'T ALWAYS WORK, BUT MOST OF THE TIME THEY ARE KILLING THE BAD GUYS.

MONTAGNARDS ARE LIKE THE AMERICAN INDIANS IN THE U.S. THEY'RE DIVIDED UP INTO A BUNCH OF DIFFERENT TRIBES--MNONG, RONGAO, RHADE, AND A COUPLE OF DOZEN OTHERS. THEY ALL HAD TO BE BROUGHT ALONG SEPARATELY.

MANIPULATING PEOPLE AND SCREWING WITH THEIR BRAINS IS THE CIA'S STOCK IN TRADE.

B-52 STRIKES, CODE NAME "ARC LIGHT". JOURNAL, YOU'RE LOOKING AT THE INFAMOUS HO CHI MINH TRAIL.

BUT THIS IS CAMBODIA, WE'RE NOT AT WAR WITH CAMBODIA!

WE'RE NOT AT WAR WITH LAOS EITHER, BUT THE SITUATION'S THE SAME UP NORTH.

SEE, WHAT THE PEOPLE AT HOME DON'T UNDERSTAND IS THAT THE HO CHI MINH TRAIL ISN'T ONE WELL-DEFINED ROAD FROM NORTH VIETNAM TO THE SOUTH. IT'S 150 MILES WIDE, THE FULL LENGTH OF LAOS AND CAMBODIA.

IT'S A MILLION TRAILS AND GOAT PATHS OVER MOUNTAINS, ACROSS RIVERS AND STREAMS. IT'S HIDDEN FOR THE MOST PART BY THE JUNGLE.

LORD!

WHUMP
WHUMP
WHUMP

EXACTLY. THAT'S WHY IT'S IMPOSSIBLE TO STOP NORTH VIETNAMESE TROOPS AND SUPPLIES FROM MOVING SOUTH.

YOUR CHEATIN' HEART... *

A SHORT WHILE LATER--CONTACT.

YELLOW RAIN, YELLOW RAIN, THIS IS *SWEET SUGAR*. DO YOU COPY? OVER.

YOU SURE THAT'S HIM?

I THINK SO. I GOT A "FIVE BY FIVE" OUT OF HIM BEFORE HE WENT TO STATIC.

YELLOW RAIN, KEY YOUR MIKE TWICE FOR IDENT, IF YOU ROGER. OVER.

I DON'T LIKE IT, MOON. *ANYBODY* COULD BE KEYING THAT MIKE.

I HEAR THAT. ON YOUR TOES, PAPA, THIS SITUATION COULD DEGENERATE REAL QUICK!

CLICK CLICK

TELL ME SOMETHING I DON'T KNOW.

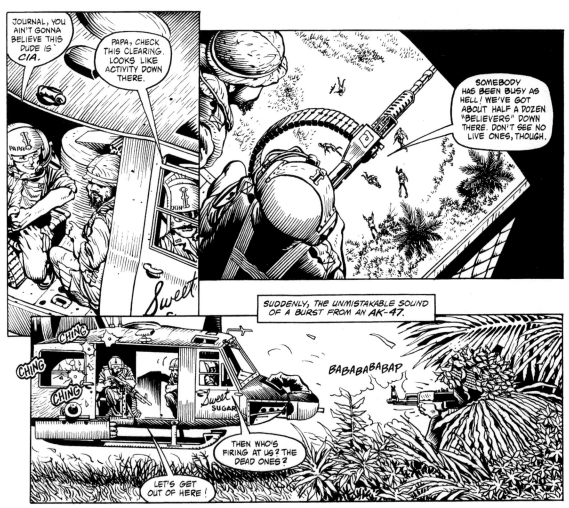

JOURNAL, YOU AIN'T GONNA BELIEVE THIS DUDE IS CIA.

PAPA, CHECK THIS CLEARING. LOOKS LIKE ACTIVITY DOWN THERE.

SOMEBODY HAS BEEN BUSY AS HELL! WE'VE GOT ABOUT HALF A DOZEN "BELIEVERS" DOWN THERE. DON'T SEE NO LIVE ONES, THOUGH.

SUDDENLY, THE UNMISTAKABLE SOUND OF A BURST FROM AN *AK-47.*

CHING

CHING

CHING

BABABABABAP

THEN WHO'S FIRING AT US? THE DEAD ONES?

LET'S GET OUT OF HERE!

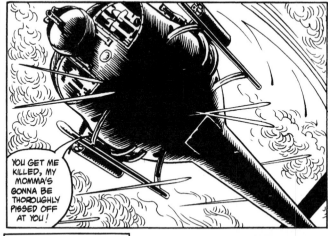

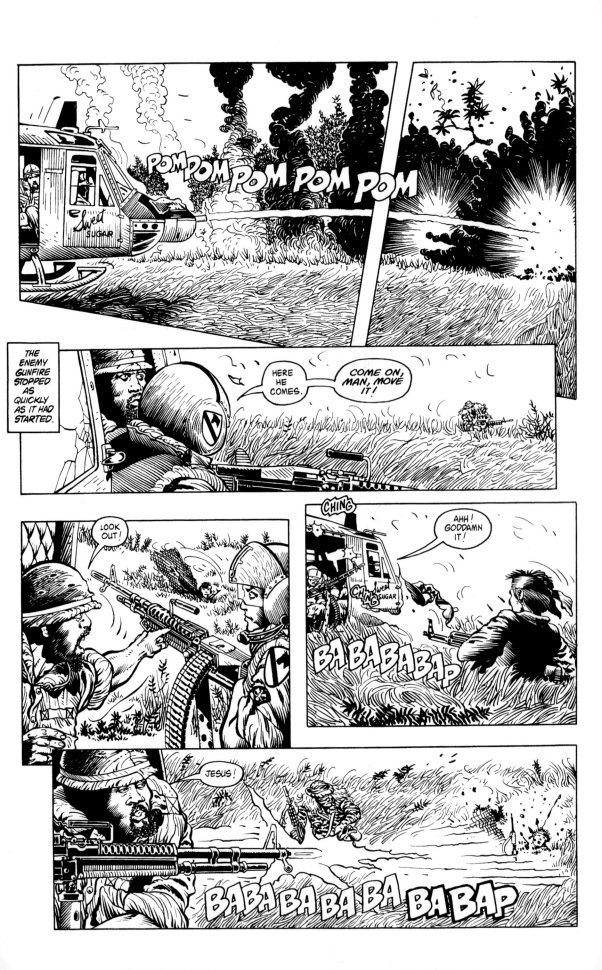

HEY, HOW'S IT GOING? NAME'S HENRY RHEIN, PARTNER. YOU LOOK LIKE A FISH OUT OF WATER.

CALL ME JOURNAL.

'YARDS CALL RHEIN "YELLOW RAIN." THEY AIN'T NEVER SEEN NOTHIN' LIKE HIM BEFORE.

WHAT ABOUT YOUR COMPANIONS?

THE RHADES? DON'T WORRY ABOUT THEM. THEY HAVE A TRICK OF MELTING AWAY.

I'VE SEEN THEM SLIP THROUGH AN ENTIRE BATTALION OF NORTH VIETNAMESE REGULARS, WHO KNEW THEY WERE THERE, MIND YOU. AND GET AWAY WITH IT.

TOKE?

NO, THANKS.

MACV (MILITARY ASSISTANCE COMMAND VIETNAM) FIELD COMMAND 5TH SPECIAL FORCES GROUP, BAN ME THUOT, 1632 HOURS.

SO, WHAT'S THE PLAN NOW?

WE WAIT UNTIL THIS BIG, CRAPOLA, HUSH-HUSH MEETING IS OVER, THEN TAKE HIM BACK AND DUMP HIM WHEREVER HE WANTS.

WELL, SPEAK OF THE DEVIL.

YOU READY TO HEAD OUT?

NO WAY, MAN, NOT 'TIL I HAVE A BEER. IT MAY BE THREE MORE MONTHS BEFORE I GET BACK TO CIVILIZATION AGAIN.

YOU CALL THIS CIVILIZATION?

WHERE YOU FROM, RHEIN?

WEST TEXAS, JUST OUTSIDE ODESSA.

GIVE ME A BEER, MOMMA-SAN.

TELL JOURNAL ABOUT THE BUCK SERGEANT WHO WAS BRAGGING TO YOU OUTSIDE.

LORDY, HE WAS A CAUTION.

HEY, YOU G.I.?

HE MUST HAVE THOUGHT I JUST GOT OFF THE BOAT.

YOU BABY-SAN? YOU BUY ME SAIGON TEA?

I PRETENDED I WAS IMPRESSED WITH HIS GREEN BERET. HE WENT ON ABOUT WHAT A TRAINED KILLER HE WAS, FEARED BY "CHARLIE" FAR AND WIDE.

MAYBE YOU "CHERRY BOY"--THAT IT?

TOLD ME HE COULD CUT A MAN'S THROAT WITHOUT A SOUND. SEE, THAT'S WHERE THE AMATEURS MAKE THEIR MISTAKE. CUTTING A MAN'S THROAT IS FAR FROM QUIET. HELL, I'VE SEEN 'EM GURGLE, THRASH AROUND, EVEN RUN AROUND BANGING INTO TREES BEFORE THEIR BRAINS RUN OUT OF OXYGEN.

YOU BOOM-BOOM 500P?

NOW, IF YOU REALLY WANT TO SHUT SOME-BODY UP, JUST GRAB 'EM LIKE THIS--

MMMPH MMMM MMM

PUT YOUR RANDALL AT THE INDENT AT THE BASE OF THE SKULL--BONE'S THIN THERE. THEN SLAM UPWARD AT A 45-DEGREE ANGLE. YOU SCRAMBLE THEIR MEDULLA OBLONGATA AND THE MOTOR SENSES ARE CUT INSTANTLY.

UH UH MMMM

THAT'S NOT FUNNY, RHEIN.

WHEN I GOT BACK TO THE BAR, RHEIN WAS ACTING AS THOUGH NOTHING HAD HAPPENED.

LET'S GO, JOURNAL. RHEIN WANTS TO GET DROPPED OFF BEFORE DARK. WE'RE ALL GASSED AND READY.

YOU MEAN YOU'RE GOING TO RISK YOUR AIRCRAFT AND CREW *AGAIN* FOR THIS PSYCHO BASTARD?

HEY, YOU DON'T HAVE TO GO IF YOU DON'T WANT. BUT THAT'S OUR JOB.

YOU STAY?

NEVERMIND, I'LL BE RIGHT BEHIND YOU.

DON'T LEAVE, I LOVE YOU! YOU NOT LOVE ME?

SORRY, LITTLE GIRL. I'VE GOT TO GO TO WORK.

HI, G.I. WE BOOM-BOOM, YOU GO PX, BUY ME JEANS?

I HAD ONCE ASKED MYSELF HOW LONG IT WOULD TAKE ME TO BECOME AS NUTS AS EVERYONE ELSE HERE. AND IF I WOULD KNOW IT WHEN IT HAPPENED. I WAS BEGINNING TO THINK I PROBABLY WOULDN'T.

THANKS, FRANK. YOU'RE A LIFE SAVER.

ROGER. WHEN YOU HURT ENOUGH TO WANT THE VERY BEST, JUST CALL *SPOOKY*, 1800 TO 0600 DAILY. WE DO IT ALL. OUT.

HOW ARE YOU DOING BACK THERE?

ALMOST FINISHED. IT SHOULD HOLD TOGETHER, BUT WE'D BETTER HEAD FOR THE NEAREST PAD.

THAT'D BE *BAN ME THUOT*.

YOU HEAR THAT, JOURNAL? THINK YOUR LITTLE BAR GIRL WILL BE HAPPY TO SEE YOU AGAIN?

HMM--

I CAN'T GET RHEIN OUT OF MY MIND.

DID THE JOB MAKE HIM THAT WAY, OR WAS HE CRAZY WHEN HE CAME HERE?

I DON'T THINK IT MATTERS MUCH. WHETHER HE'S A PRODUCT OF THE SYSTEM OR OF THE LIFE HE LEADS, IT'S *HIS* CHOICE.

THE BOYS UPSTAIRS LOVE HIM. *ANY* SHADY, FILTHY JOB IS RIGHT UP HIS ALLEY.

I WONDER WHAT HE'S TRYING TO PROVE?

GOING UP.

SATURDAY, MARCH 18, 1967. 0542 HOURS. III CORPS, WAR ZONE C, IN THE MIDDLE OF THE *IRON TRIANGLE*, NORTHWEST OF *SAIGON*. THE RAIN HAD LESSENED TO A DRIZZLE DURING THE NIGHT, ONLY TO BE REPLACED BY AN EVER-THICKENING FOG.

MY TENSION EASED AS THE WEATHER CLOSED IN AROUND US. THE IDEA THAT, "IF THEY CAN'T SEE ME, THEY CAN'T SHOOT ME," GAVE ME A MEASURE OF SECURITY, HOWEVER FALSE IT MIGHT PROVE TO BE.

COMMO

YOU FEELIN' ANY BETTER, JOURNAL?

SOME BETTER, TEED. I JUST FILED MY STORY ON THE DEATH OF CORPORAL STYLES, BUT I CAN'T SHAKE THE SICKNESS IN MY GUT.

YOU'VE SEEN PEOPLE DIE BEFORE. AFTER ALL, YOU'VE BEEN A WAR CORRESPONDENT FOR TWELVE YEARS.

YEAH, BUT THIS WAR SEEMS DIFFERENT. VAGUE, MEANINGLESS, WITHOUT PURPOSE.

JEEZ, I HOPE HEMINGWAY DIDN'T HEAR THAT. BESIDES, *I'M* THE ONE WHO PUT STYLES IN HARM'S WAY. IF ANYONE SHOULD FEEL GUILTY ABOUT HIS DEATH, IT SHOULD BE ME.

DO YOU?

I CAN'T AFFORD IT.

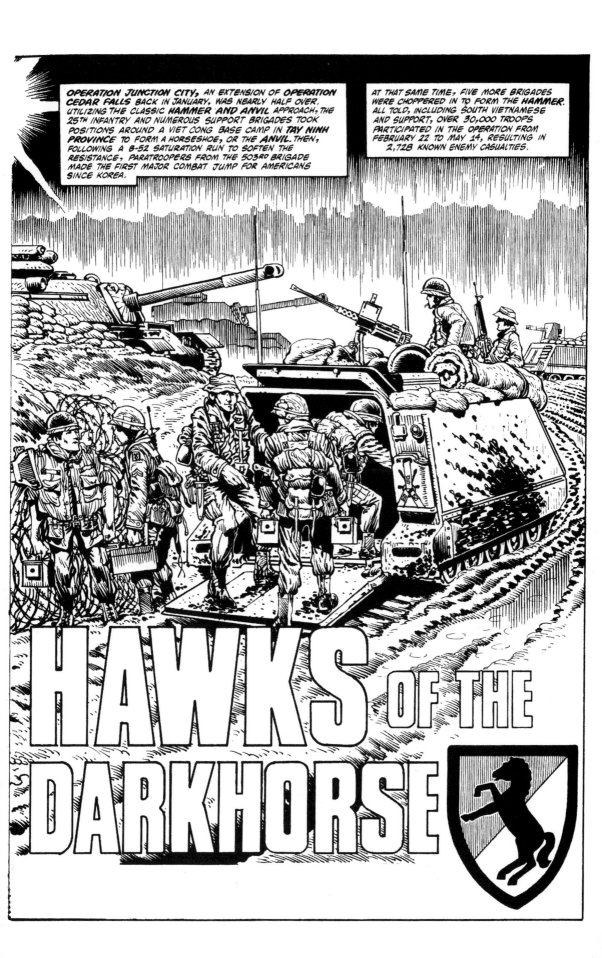

OPERATION JUNCTION CITY, AN EXTENSION OF OPERATION CEDAR FALLS BACK IN JANUARY, WAS NEARLY HALF OVER. UTILIZING THE CLASSIC HAMMER AND ANVIL APPROACH, THE 25TH INFANTRY AND NUMEROUS SUPPORT BRIGADES TOOK POSITIONS AROUND A VIET CONG BASE CAMP IN TAY NINH PROVINCE TO FORM A HORSESHOE, OR THE ANVIL. THEN, FOLLOWING A B-52 SATURATION RUN TO SOFTEN THE RESISTANCE, PARATROOPERS FROM THE 503RD BRIGADE MADE THE FIRST MAJOR COMBAT JUMP FOR AMERICANS SINCE KOREA.

AT THAT SAME TIME, FIVE MORE BRIGADES WERE CHOPPERED IN TO FORM THE HAMMER. ALL TOLD, INCLUDING SOUTH VIETNAMESE AND SUPPORT, OVER 30,000 TROOPS PARTICIPATED IN THE OPERATION FROM FEBRUARY 22 TO MAY 14, RESULTING IN 2,728 KNOWN ENEMY CASUALTIES.

HAWKS OF THE DARKHORSE

IT'S GOING TO BE HARD FLYING AROUND IN THAT SOUP OUT THERE TODAY, WON'T IT?

WE LIVE FOR HARD, TEED. WE'RE HARD ALL OVER!

YEAH, MAN, WE'RE *HAWKS OF THE DARKHORSE,* ASSKICKERS SUPREME!

THINGS ARE GONNA BE KINDA DULL AROUND HERE TODAY. YOU WANNA RIDE ALONG WITH US?

MAYBE. I'LL THINK ABOUT IT.

REMEMBER, JAMES DEAN DIED FOR YOUR SINS.

MY GOD, THEY'RE JUST KIDS!

YEAH, SCOUT PILOTS ARE ALL YOUNG. YOU DON'T GET OLD IN THEIR LINE OF WORK.

BILL DAVIS IS THE OLDEST COMMISSIONED OFFICER IN HIS PLATOON, AND HE'S ONLY 21. THEY'VE GOT THE MOST DANGEROUS, NERVEWRACKING JOB IN THE ARMY!

THERE ARE 15 PILOTS IN THEIR PLATOON. THEY'VE LOST 38 KILLED OR WOUNDED-- AN ATTRITION RATE OF MORE THAN 250%!

THEY HAVE A TENDENCY TO LIVE HARD.

AND DIE YOUNG?

MAYBE I WILL RIDE WITH THEM TODAY, SEE WHAT MAKES THEM TICK.

LOTSA LUCK. I LIKE TO KEEP BOTH FEET ON THE GROUND. IT'S HARD TO "DIG IN" UP THERE-- COVER IS SCARCE!

I'M READY WHEN YOU ARE.

AAAEEEOOOO, CHERRY BOY!

ALL RIGHT, WELCOME TO THE UNFRIENDLY SKIES OF VIETNAM. WE'RE OUTTA HERE!

AFTER MY FIRST GLIMPSE OF THE OH-6 CAYUSE THAT THESE AERO SCOUTS FLEW, I BEGAN TO HAVE SECOND THOUGHTS.

MY GOD, IT'S TINY!

YEAH, WELL, THE SMALLER THE PACKAGE, THE HARDER IT IS TO HIT.

WITH A "FREE" M-60 ON THE STARBOARD DOOR AND A MINI-GUN ON THE PORT SIDE, WE'VE GOT QUITE A STING FOR OUR SIZE.

WE USUALLY "TROLL" FOR A "HEAVY HOG" OF THE 3RD SQUADRON--THAT'S A CHARLIE MODEL HUEY ARMED TO THE TEETH. BUT IT'S DOWN FOR REPAIRS.

YEAH, WE COME IN LOW AND SLOW OVER A SUSPECTED ENEMY AREA TO DRAW FIRE WHILE THE GUNSHIP HANGS BACK WAITING. WHEN THE VC OPEN UP ON US, WE KICK OUT A SMOKE GRENADE AND DI-DI THE AREA ASAP WHILE THE HUEY UNLOADS ON CHUCKLES, MAKIN' BELIEVERS OUT OF 'EM.

OUR JOB IS A LITTLE DIFFERENT TODAY. WE'LL BE FLYING ALONE, SPOTTING FOR THE AIR FORCE. OUR MISSION WILL BE TO FIX ENEMY POSITIONS, NOT TO ENGAGE. IF THE TARGET IS HOT, WE CALL IN FAST MOVERS TO NAPALM THE AREA.

BUT FIRST, IF WE'LL ALL BOW OUR HEADS FOR A MINUTE TO REMEMBER OUR FELLOW TROOPERS WHO'VE GONE BEFORE US...

WE STOOD SILENTLY, EACH REFLECTING IN HIS OWN WAY. GONE WAS THE ADOLESCENT JOKING. THESE YOUNG MEN TOOK THEIR JOB SERIOUSLY, AFTER ALL.

THE CREW REFERRED TO THE TINY HELICOPTER AS A *"LOACH"*-- LIGHT OBSERVATION HELICOPTER. THE FOUR-BLADED ROTOR PROVIDED A MUCH SMOOTHER RIDE THAN THE HUEY. WE LIFTED OFF INTO THE DISMAL MORNING SKY.

WE HAVE A LITTLE ERRAND TO RUN FIRST. PICK UP SOME MAJOR AND DELIVER HIM TO BRIGADE. IT SHOULDN'T TAKE OVER HALF AN HOUR.

YOU LIKE THE *"FREE"* M-60 BETTER THAN THE FIXED-MOUNT TYPE?

OH, YEAH. YOU GOT A LOT MORE FREEDOM OF MOVEMENT WITH THE BUNGI STRAP.

WHERE YOU FROM?

EAST PEORIA, ILLINOIS. RAISED WITH THE CATERPILLAR TRACTOR COMPANY IN MY BACK YARD. I GOT A JOB THERE TO GO BACK TO.

WE WERE ONLY IN THE AIR ABOUT FIFTEEN MINUTES WHEN --

THERE SHOULD BE A RIDGE COMING UP, THE VILLAGE SHOULD BE JUST ON THE OTHER SIDE OF IT. DAMN VISIBILITY CAN'T BE MORE THAN A QUARTER OF A MILE.

I WAS AMAZED BY WILD BILL'S DEAD RECKONING.

OVER THERE, BILL. THAT FIELD LOOKS LIKE A GOOD SPOT.

BLAM BLAM BLAM BLAM BLAM
CLICK CLICK

COME ON, WADE, COME ON, OLD BUDDY, IT'S OVER.

LET'S GO, BRO.

I DON'T KNOW, MAN. PART OF ME WANTED HIM TO DO IT, AND PART OF ME DIDN'T.

I GUESS THIS IS ONE OF THOSE TIMES THAT IT'S HELL IF YOU DO, AND HELL IF YOU DON'T.

BLAM BLAM BLAM

COME ON, I GOTTA LOCATE THAT MAJOR.

AT THE COMMAND POST--

ARE YOU CAPTAIN DAVIS' CREW CHIEF?

YESSIR.

WE HAVE A SQUAD HEADING OVER TO SECURE HIS AIRCRAFT. TELL HIM TO GET OVER HERE ASAP. NOW, SPECIALIST, *MOVE!*

RIGHT AWAY, SIR!

HANG HERE, I'LL BE RIGHT BACK. THERE GOES OUR QUIET DAY, AS USUAL.

MAJOR VORSANGER HAD A "SITUATION" ON HIS HANDS. A PLATOON WAS TAKING FIRE FROM A LARGE CONTINGENT OF VC. BUT NOBODY KNEW WHERE THEY WERE.

LIEUTENANT KRACHT IS DOWN AND DISORIENTED, AS CLOSE AS WE CAN TELL, THEY'RE IN THIS AREA, HERE.

THEY'RE GOING TO BE DAMN HARD TO SPOT IN THAT TERRAIN. IT'S ROUGHER THAN HELL IN THERE.

THAT SHOULDN'T BE A PROBLEM. I TOLD THEM TO KEEP IN CONSTANT CONTACT WITH YOU.

LET'S DO IT!

RIGHT. YOU JUST SPOT THEM AND GET OUT. WE HAVE A CHINOOK ORDERED UP. HE SHOULD BE HERE IN HALF AN HOUR.

TELL HIM TO HOLD UNTIL WE DO OUR THING. I DON'T WANT TO FLY INTO HIM IN THE FOG.

BA BA BA BAP

WHIRRR

WE BURST OVER THE TREE TOPS JUST SECONDS BEFORE YANKEE WHISKEY WOULD HAVE BEEN OVERRUN.

BADAP DAP DAP

WHIR RRR

FLAHERTY'S ACCURACY WAS AMAZING. SOME OF HIS ROUNDS IMPACTED ONLY FEET FROM OUR TROOPS!

ENEMY SURVIVORS SCRAMBLED BACK DOWN THE GORGE!

IN SECONDS WE WERE OUT OF SIGHT BEHIND THE TREES, THAT WE WERE STILL ALIVE WAS DUE TO THE FANTASTIC MANEUVER-ABILITY OF THE LOACH.

THE NEXT FIVE OR SIX MINUTES SEEMED LIKE HOURS.

DAVIS MOVED THE TINY HELO FROM SIDE TO SIDE ERRATICALLY TO DODGE THE GROUND FIRE AS FLAHERTY FIRED SMALL ACCURATE BURSTS TO CONSERVE AMMO.

WHIRRRR

SPEC-4 BODIAN WAS MORE OUTSIDE THE CHOPPER THAN IN.

THEN--

THUD

THUD

UHH--

BODIAN!

GRAB HIM! JOURNAL!

GOT HIM!

THERE WAS BLOOD EVERYWHERE, FRANTICALLY, I SEARCHED FOR THE SOURCE.

HOW BAD?

OH, DAMMIT-- DAMMIT!

I CAN'T BELIEVE THIS THING IS STILL FLYING.

THERE-- OVER THERE. SEE THEM?

YEAH, I SEE THEM!

AS THE MACHINE GUN BUCKED AGAINST ME--

--THE HORROR OF WHAT I WAS DOING RECEDED. THE 60 BECAME A WARM, FRIENDLY THING. THAT FEELING WILL HAUNT ME UNTIL THE DAY I DIE.

THEY'RE ALL ON THE LADDER, MY GOD--WE'RE GONNA DO IT!

WE'RE GONNA PULL IT OFF!

YOU GOT 'EM ALL, BIG BOPPER. HOTEL ALPHA!

AND "HAUL ASS" HE DID, WITH EIGHT TROOPERS CLINGING PRECARIOUSLY TO JACOB'S LADDER.

MAKE SURE YOU GO AT LEAST FIVE KLICKS UP THE VALLEY BEFORE HANGING A RIGHT, BIG BOPPER. THERE IS ONE HELL OF A MOUNTAIN DIRECTLY TO YOUR STARBOARD SIDE.

LET'S GET THE HELL OUT OF HERE!

BADAP BADAP DAP DAP DAP

WE'RE GONE, JOURNAL!

HOW ABOUT IT, BIG BOPPER? DID YOU COPY THAT?

BABABABABAP

THERE WAS A NOTICEABLE EDGE IN DAVIS' VOICE AS HE REPEATED--

BIG BOPPER, BIG BOPPER, THIS IS RUM RUNNER, DO YOU ROGER?

MAYBE THEIR RADIO'S OUT.

YEAH, MAYBE.

BIG BOPPER, BIG BOPPER, ACKNOWLEDGE

I TURNED MY ATTENTION TO BANDAGING THE CO-PILOT'S LEGS AS THE LOACH LIMPED THROUGH THE FOG.

NONE OF US WOULD ADMIT WHAT WE FEARED.

tradition

WE WERE PINNED DOWN. RETRACING OUR ROUTE BACK ACROSS THE OPEN RICE PADDIES WOULD BE SUICIDE.

TANGO-26 TO MAY-FLOWER, SUSTAINING HEAVY ENEMY FIRE! REQUEST ARTILLERY ON MY MARK! TWO-NINER-TWO BY ZERO-FIVE-EIGHT...

WONDERFUL, THEY PICK THIS PARTICULAR TIME TO MOVE! THEY'RE HANGING OUT OVER THE BOONIES SOME DAMN PLACE!

WWOOOOOOSSHH

WHO THE HELL FIRED THAT *LAW?* KNOCK IT OFF -- CALM DOWN!

THREE SHOT BURSTS. THAT'S IT, CALM DOWN. CONSERVE YOUR AMMO, WE MAY BE HERE A WHILE.

DOW DOW

YOU O.K., JOURNAL?

I THINK SO.

CHUNG

WISH YOU WERE BACK IN SAIGON KISSING WESTMORELAND'S BRASS?

YOU WANT THE TRUTH? YES.

SARGE, THEY'RE RUSHING US!

FTA ALL THE WAY

A DOZEN SHAPES BROKE COVER, RUNNING ALONG A DRY DITCH TOWARD US.

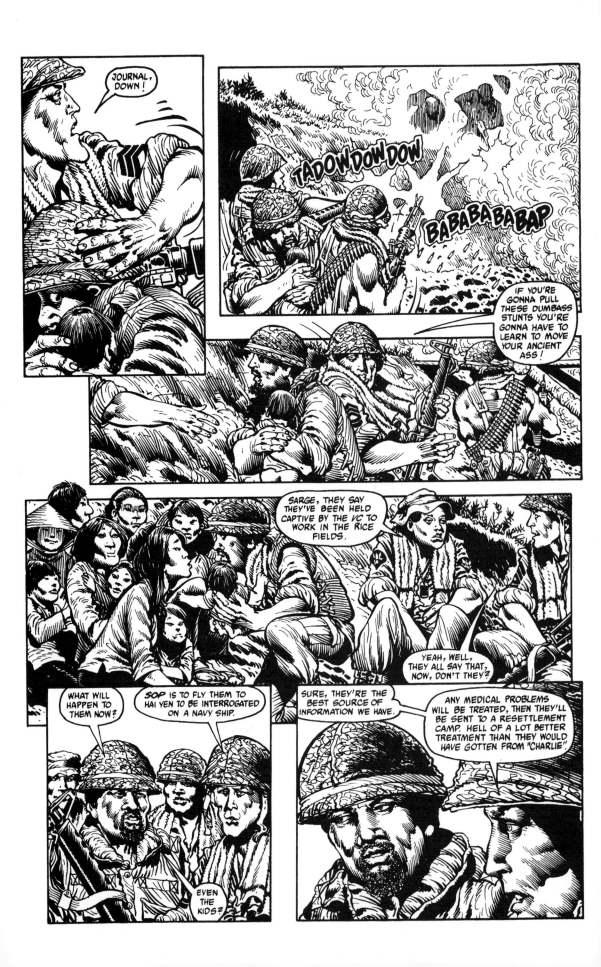

IT HAD BEEN ABOUT 20 MINUTES SINCE THE AIR STRIKE AND THERE HAD BEEN NO MOVEMENT FROM THE VILLAGE.

HERE COME THE APC'S, SARGE.

YOU GOT INDIGENOUS PERSONNEL TO EVACUATE, SERGEANT?

ANDERSON, LOAD 'EM UP.

YOU TAKE GOOD CARE OF THIS ONE. I GUESS SHE'S ALL ALONE NOW.

NOT TO WORRY.

UH UH UH

IT'S OK, SWEETHEART.

WAA WAAA

I GUESS IT TAKES SOMETHING LIKE THIS TO MAKE ME REALIZE HOW FAR BACK THIS CIVILIZATION GOES.

THOUSANDS OF YEARS OF TRADITION. THAT'S WHY IT'S SO DAMNED ARROGANT OF US TO TRY TO FORCE THESE PEOPLE TO LIVE THEIR LIVES ON OUR TERMS.

WE CALL THIS A BACKWARD COUNTRY. I WONDER HOW FAR WE WOULD HAVE COME IF WE HAD BEEN AT WAR FOR 4,000 YEARS LIKE THEY'VE BEEN WITH THE CHINESE.

SOME FOLKS SAY THAT THEY'RE ALWAYS AT WAR BECAUSE THEY DON'T KNOW ANYTHING ELSE.

I DON'T BELIEVE THAT CRAP!

THEY ARE A SWEET, LOVING PEOPLE WHO JUST WANT TO LIVE THEIR LIVES, RAISE THEIR BABIES, AND GROW SOME RICE.

YOU'RE A PARADOX, TEED ...A CAREER SOLDIER WITH A CONSCIENCE.

OH, GET OFF IT! ANYONE CAN SEE THE STUPIDITY HERE--ON BOTH SIDES. I'M A PROFESSIONAL SOLDIER, JOURNAL--

FRONT TOWARD ENEMY

--BUT I'M ALSO A HUMAN-GODDAMN-BEING! TWENTY YEARS AND I'M OUT. THEN I'M MOVING INTO THE BACK-WOODS AS FAR AWAY FROM THE PHONIES AND THE POLITICIANS AS I CAN GET.

SOUNDS GOOD TO ME.

I DIDN'T HAVE THE HEART TO TELL HIM I'D BEEN THERE. THERE IS NO PLACE TO HIDE.

ANDERSON, DIG IN UP BEHIND THAT RISE AND SET UP THE 60 UP THERE.

I TRIED IT ONCE, BUT I CARRIED IT ALL WITH ME, INSIDE. I GUESS THAT'S WHY I'M BACK, REPORTING ON THE THING I HATE MOST IN LIFE--*WAR*.

AND I DIDN'T BELIEVE TEED WHEN HE SAID THAT HE DIDN'T CARE, EITHER.

SOLDANO, HOVEY, SET A COUPLE CLAYMORES ON BOTH SIDES OF THAT CRACK, THEY MIGHT TRY THAT APPROACH.

WE WERE PRETTY WELL DUG IN BY NIGHTFALL.

GOD, I HATE THE NIGHT OVER HERE.

YEAH, I KNOW WHAT YOU MEAN. WHAT'S FOR SUPPER, JOURNAL?

LOOKS LIKE BEANY WEENIES. YOU WANT THE SMOKES?

YEAH. YOU WANT A POUND CAKE?

YEAH, THANKS, WISH WE COULD STRIKE A FIRE, I COULD USE A WARM CUP OF COFFEE.

WHUMP WHUMP WHUMP

WHUMP WHUMP WHUMP

JESUS! LIEUTENANT! GOT ONE ALIVE OVER HERE!

THIS OL' BOY HAS GOT SOME MAJOR HEAD DAMAGE. WE WON'T BE ABLE TO FIND OUT HOW MUCH UNTIL WE TAKE SOME X-RAYS. CALL FOR A DUSTOFF, SIR.

HE KEEPS MUTTERING SOMETHING ABOUT PUSAN. WHERE THE HELL IS PUSAN?

PUSAN IS IN KOREA. HE THINKS HE'S BACK FIGHTING THE KOREAN WAR.

WELL, I GUESS ONE WAR IS AS GOOD AS THE NEXT.

AMERICAN INVOLVEMENT VIETNAM

BONG SON

PLEIKU • AN KHE

IA DRANG VALLEY

QUI NHON

SOUTH VIETNAM • TUY HOA

IA DRANG VALLEY: THE FIRST MAJOR CONTACT

ON SEPTEMBER 15, 1965 THE *FIRST AIR CAVALRY* ARRIVED IN *VIETNAM* DIVISION STRENGTH, 16000 TROOPS, AND SET UP OPERATIONS AT *AN KHE* IN THE CENTRAL HIGHLANDS.

THEIR BAPTISM UNDER FIRE CAME QUICKLY. AT THAT SAME TIME THE *NORTH VIETNAMESE POLITBURO* DIRECTED THREE REGIMENTS OF NVA REGULARS (THE 32ND, 33RD, AND 66TH) TO CUT *SOUTH VIETNAM* IN HALF BY PUSHING EAST TO THE SEA.

ON OCTOBER 19, 1965 THE NVA BEGAN THEIR OFFENSIVE BY ATTACKING THE SPECIAL FORCES CAMP AT *PLEI ME*, 25 MILES SOUTHWEST OF *PLEIKU*.

TRUE TO TRADITION, THE CAVALRY SHADOWED THE FLEEING *NORTH VIETNAMESE 33RD'S* SURVIVORS, UNTIL THEY REGROUPED WITH THE 66TH REGIMENT IN THE *IA DRANG VALLEY.*

430 MEN OF THE FIRST CAVALRY (2ND BN OF THE 7TH CAV, AIRMOBILE INFANTRY) WERE HELICOPTERED INTO AN L.Z. IN THE *IA DRANG VALLEY.*

FIGHTING WAS INTENSE, OFTEN *HAND TO HAND!*

THEIR SURVIVAL WOULD HAVE BEEN DOUBTFUL IF IT WERE NOT FOR THE AIR SUPPORT OF B-52 SATURATION BOMBING. 344 TONS OF BOMBS WERE DROPPED ON NOVEMBER 14 ALONE!

WHILE INTENSIVE ARTILLERY SATURATION ENABLED THE FIRST BATTALION TO STAND THEIR GROUND.

ON NOVEMBER 15 THE SECOND BATTALION OF THE FIFTH CAVALRY LANDED AT AN L.Z. TWO AND A HALF MILES SOUTHEAST.

MOVING OVERLAND THEY REINFORCED THE BELEAGUERED FIRST BN AND GRADUALLY BEGAN TO GET THE UPPER HAND.

THE TURNING POINT CAME WHEN THE INFANTRY LOCATED THE MAIN NVA BASE CAMP AT THE FOOT OF THE CHU PONG MOUNTAINS.

DAILY B-52 SATURATION DUMPED NEARLY 2000 TONS OF BOMBS ON THE POSITION BREAKING THE BACK OF THE NVA RESISTANCE.

BATTERED SURVIVORS ESCAPED ACROSS THE BORDER INTO *CAMBODIA*. ENEMY DEAD TOTALED 1771.

OFFICIALLY DESIGNATED *"SILVER BAYONET"* THE BATTLE OF THE *IA DRANG VALLEY* TAUGHT AMERICANS MUCH ABOUT THEIR NEW ENEMY. NO BAREFOOT PEASANTS THESE...THEY WERE TOUGH, SAVAGE, AND PROFESSIONAL. THIS FIRST BATTLE HINTED THAT IT WOULD BE A LONG WAR.

IRONICALLY, TEN YEARS LATER THE *NORTH VIETNAMESE* WOULD START THEIR *LAST OFFENSIVE* TO OVERRUN THE SOUTH NEAR THE *IA DRANG VALLEY* WITH THEIR ATTACK ON *BAN ME THUOT,* MARCH 10, 1975.

the 5.56 BLUES

POLICY AFFIRMED

PRESIDENT, IN NASHVILLE TALK, SAYS U.S. WILL "STAY THE COURSE"

by Roy Reed

Special to the New York Times

NASHVILLE, Tenn., March 15

President Johnson chose this Upper South capital, with its long tradition of patriotism and military pride, for a strong defense and reassertion of his Vietnam policy today.

"America is committed to the defense of South Vietnam until an honorable peace can be negotiated," he said with emphasis, adding that if this point got through to the other side, peace talks could start at once.

He made a lengthy justification of the bombing of North Vietnam, repeated his willingness to end the war if the other side would show the same willingness and expressed his firm determination to "stay the course."

Officials at the War...

IN THE EARLY MONTHS OF 1967, AMERICAN TROOP STRENGTH IN SOUTH VIETNAM ROSE TO OVER 400,000 MEN, MARKING A TURNING POINT IN U.S. STRATEGY. UNDER THE COMMAND OF GENERAL WESTMORELAND, THE LIMITED WAR STRATEGIES OF 1965 AND 1966 GAVE WAY TO THE YEAR OF LARGE-SCALE SEARCH AND DESTROY MISSIONS.

WITH 5,000 AMERICANS ALREADY DEAD AND OVER 30,000 WOUNDED, JUST STAYING ALIVE UNTIL HIS ROTATION DATE WAS THE AVERAGE G.I.'S MAIN OBJECTIVE.

OPERATION JUNCTION CITY, WAR ZONE "C", NORTHWEST OF SAIGON, NEAR THE CAMBODIAN BORDER.

I DUNNO WHY THEY CALL THEM SAND BAGS--I AIN'T NEVER SEEN NOBODY PUT NOTHIN' BUT MUD IN THE DAMN THINGS SINCE I CAME TO 'NAM.

HEY, JOURNAL, HOW'D YOU GET SUCKERED INTO MANUAL LABOR?

STYLES PROMISED ME ONE OF HIS FAMOUS "HOME COOKED MEALS" IF I'D HELP.

WHAT? THIS GOD-AWFUL PORK SUET'N' NOODLES WIT' THE BRICK-BAT BISCUIT?

EAT YOUR HEART OUT, WESTLEY. IT'S AN HONEST-TO-GOODNESS B-6 UNIT. THE ONE WIT' THE FRUIT COCKTAIL.

SARGE, STYLES THINKS JUST 'CAUSE HE'S A GODDAMN CORPORAL HE CAN COMMANDEER THE BEST C-RATIONS.

QUIT WHINING AND DIG, WESTLEY. IF YOU DON'T HAVE YOUR POSITION SECURED BY NIGHTFALL, IT'S YOUR ASS THAT'LL BE SHOT OFF, NOT MINE!

MAJOR LOSS TO THE COMPANY AND MANKIND.

STYLES, GRAB THE RT AND FOLLOW ME.

NO. OH NO, SARGE, IT CAN'T BE MY TURN. I'M TOO SHORT FOR THIS CRAP.

WHAT IS IT? WHERE ARE YOU GOING?

TO SET UP A LISTENING POST OUTSIDE THE PERIMETER. MIGHT AS WELL PUT OUT A SIGN SAYING "YOO-HOO, CHARLIE, PLEASE BLOW THIS DUMBASS AWAY."

YOU WANT TO BE AN NCO, YOU TAKE YOUR TURN LIKE EVERYBODY ELSE. PRIVILEGE OF RANK.

THIS LOOKS GOOD. DIG IN HERE AND SET YOUR TRIP FLARES 50 METERS OUT.

YES, MOTHER.

LISTEN, STYLES, DON'T TRY TO BE A HERO. THE FIRST SIGN OF ACTIVITY, YOU GET YOUR SORRY ASS BACK INSIDE THE PERIMETER-- UNDERSTOOD?

JUST MAKE SURE EVERYONE KNOWS I'M OUT HERE. I DON'T WANT TO GIVE WESTLEY AN EXCUSE.

MIND IF I KEEP YOU COMPANY?

SURE, IT'S YOUR FUNERAL.

YOU GOT A DEATH WISH? OR DON'T YOU THINK YOU CAN BE KILLED?

WHEN YOU GET TO BE MY AGE, YOU KNOW IT CAN HAPPEN.

44 DAYS LEFT. I MAKE A LOT OF NOISE ABOUT ROTATING OUT OF HERE, BUT YOU KNOW WHAT? LIKE THE GUY SAYS, "YOU CAN'T GO HOME NO MORE."

THIS IS YOUR SECOND TOUR, ISN'T IT?

YEAH--AFTER MY FIRST TOUR I WENT HOME TO MY CLASS REUNION, CLASS OF '62. IT WAS WEIRD.

MY HIGH SCHOOL FRIENDS ALL KNEW I HAD BEEN TO 'NAM.

MY GOD, MAN, THEY TREATED ME LIKE I HAD THE PLAGUE. I WAS SITTING AT A PICNIC TABLE BY MYSELF AND A LITTLE GIRL CAME UP AND SMILED AT ME. HER MOTHER GRABBED HER AWAY TO A SAFE DISTANCE, AS IF I MASSACRED BABIES FOR KICKS!

I COULD SEE IT IN THEIR EYES. MAYBE THAT'S WHAT THEY SAW IN MINE. MAYBE THEY'RE RIGHT.

WE SET THE TRIP FLARES AND SOON WE WERE BACK TO THE DEBATABLE SECURITY OF STYLES' FOXHOLE.

YOU DON'T BELIEVE IN TAKING CHANCES, DO YOU? WHAT'S THAT, AN M-3 GREASE GUN? DON'T YOU TRUST YOUR M-16?

NOT HARDLY!

OVERJOYED? I WAS DESTROYED.

I JUST SAT THERE COMPARING. THE MORE I COMPARED, THE SICKER I GOT!

BACK IN '65, DURING MY FIRST TOUR, MY PLATOON HAD THE BAD LUCK TO BE ONE OF THE FIRST IN OUR BRIGADE TO BE FORCED TO TRADE IN OUR M-14'S FOR THESE "MATTEL TOYS."

I TAKE IT YOU WEREN'T OVERJOYED?

"THEY BRAGGED ABOUT HOW THE 5.56mm AMMUNITION WAS EQUALLY DEADLY BUT SMALLER THAN THE 7.62mm NATO ROUND OF THE M-14. WE COULD CARRY MORE AMMO.

"IT WAS SMALLER, ALL RIGHT!"

STYLES   U.S. ARMY

"THEY WENT ON AND ON ABOUT HOW LUCKY WE WERE TO GET 'EM, BUT IT DIDN'T SEEM LIKE A FAIR TRADE TO ME.

"I WAS TRADING A HEFTY STEEL BUTT THAT COULD KILL A MAN WITH ONE QUICK VERTICAL STROKE--

"--FOR A PLASTIC POP GUN."

"ACCORDING TO THE MANUALS, M-16'S REQUIRED LESS CLEANING THAN OTHER WEAPONS, SO THE ARMY OVERLOOKED SUPPLYING CLEANING GEAR.

"BEFORE LONG, MY SUSPICIONS WERE PROVEN RIGHT.

"WE WERE ON A 'BROWSE 'N' BUTCHER' IN QUANG NGAI PROVINCE WHEN OUR PATROL RAN HEADLONG INTO AN NVA AMBUSH.

CHA DAP DAP DAP

"DISENGAGING A SUPERIOR ENEMY FORCE BURNS UP A LOT OF AMMO--AND THE ENEMY KEPT COMING.

"WE WERE CARRYING OUR USUAL 820-ROUND ISSUE AS WE TRIED TO LEAP-FROG OUT OF THE FIREFIGHT. THEN THE MALFUNCTIONS STARTED.

BABABA
=CLANK=

"MORE AND MORE OF OUR PEOPLE WERE LEFT WITH A JAMMED WEAPON THAT DIDN'T EVEN MAKE A DECENT CLUB.

PEOW

SMAT
THUD
"I LOST A LOT OF FRIENDS THAT DAY."
PEOW

TANGO FOXTROT, THIS IS ZULU NINER. YOU GOTTA HELP US OUT WITH SUPPRESSIVE FIRE WHILE WE *DI DI* THE AREA. WE HAVE PEOPLE DOWN!

"*WE* WERE LUCKY. IF THE *UTTCO* CHOPPER HADN'T BEEN IN THE AREA TO THUMP THE GOOKS, I WOULDN'T BE *HERE* FER SURE!

"AS IT WAS, ONLY SIX OF OUR PLATOON WALKED OUT VERTICAL!

"BUT, HELL, OUR GOVERNMENT DON'T MAKE MISTAKES. SO, THE CHANGEOVER FROM M-14'S TO M-16'S CONTINUED."

'COURSE, WE KNOW NOW THAT IF THEY'RE KEPT CLEAN AND THE GAS TUBES UNOBSTRUCTED, THEY'RE FAIRLY RELIABLE. BUT I'LL NEVER BE ABLE TO TRUST MY LIFE TO ONE OF THEM AGAIN.

UNTIL RECENTLY TROOPS HAD TO HAVE THEIR FOLKS BACK IN THE WORLD SEND THEM .22 CALIBRE CLEANING RODS IN PACKAGES WITH "POGEY BAIT" JUST TO KEEP THEIR SONS ALIVE!

LATER.

I HATE THE RAIN. DINKS CAN COME RIGHT UP ON TOP OF YOU AND YOU CAN'T HEAR THEM. THE NIGHT BELONGS TO "CHARLIE."

THAT'S WHY, EVEN WITH ALL THIS MECHANIZED AIR MOBILITY, WE DON'T GET ANYWHERE. YOU CAN'T FIGHT A DEFENSIVE WAR.

"CHARLIE'S" OUT THERE LAUGHING HIS HEAD OFF 'CAUSE HE'S THE ONE WHO KNOWS WHERE AND WHEN AND *IF* THE NEXT ATTACK IS GOING TO HAPPEN.

GET DOWN! IT'S GONNA HIT THE FAN!

POP!

PYRON, GET ME TEED! I GOT CONTACT--DO IT, MAN!

CLICK

CHRIST, MAN, IT'S A GODDAMN COW!

JULY, 1967. *THE SUMMER OF LOVE*. QUITE A PARADOX, EVEN FOR THE PSEUDO-INTELLECTUALS, CONSIDERING THE HORROR GOING ON IN SOUTHEAST ASIA.

MY HEADACHES HAD CONTINUED UNABATED THESE PAST THREE MONTHS SINCE MY SURGERY FOR A HEAD INJURY IN VIETNAM. I WAS BEGINNING TO WONDER IF THEY WOULD *EVER* EASE.

MY FORMER WIFE HAD REMARRIED RECENTLY. I DIDN'T BLAME HER-- I HADN'T BEEN MUCH OF A HUSBAND DURING THE TEN YEARS WE WERE MARRIED, AND I HAD BEEN EVEN LESS OF A FATHER TO MY EIGHT-YEAR-OLD DAUGHTER, TINA.

NO MORE WAR

JANICE GOT THE HOUSE IN THE DIVORCE SETTLEMENT. A HOTEL ROOM IS NO PLACE TO CONDUCT A MEANINGFUL RELATIONSHIP WITH A LITTLE GIRL, AT LEAST THAT'S THE EXCUSE I USED. IT'S EASIER TO WALLOW IN SELF-PITY THAN TO FIX IT.

CIB

THE GRUNTS CALL IT THE 1,000 YARD STARE. I CAUGHT MYSELF STARING, QUITE OFTEN--OUT THE WINDOW, OR AT A LIGHT BULB, OR BLANKLY INTO THE DARK--MY MIND ON OVERLOAD.

ONE MORNING AROUND THE FIRST OF THE MONTH, I WOKE UP AND THE FOG HAD LIFTED. THE HEADACHES WERE GONE. I CALLED JANICE AND, TO MY SURPRISE, SHE AGREED TO ALLOW TINA TO VISIT ME THROUGHOUT THE MONTH OF JULY. ONE OF THE FEW TIMES WE EVER SAW EYE-TO-EYE ON ANYTHING.

IT WAS UNDOUBTEDLY THE MOST DELIGHTFUL MONTH OF MY LIFE.

MY BELONGINGS, MOST OF THEM STILL IN PACKING BOXES, WERE A NEVER-ENDING SOURCE OF FASCINATION FOR TINA. SHE HAD BEEN THROUGH EVERY BOX AND WAS NOW GOING THROUGH MY DESK DRAWERS.

DON'T YOU THINK YOU SHOULD FINISH YOUR FRENCH FRIES, BUTTON?

YOU CAN EAT THEM, POPPY.

CAPTIVATED BY MYSTERY, SHE WAS INEVITABLY ATTRACTED TO A JUNK-FILLED CIGAR BOX I HAD LONG SINCE SET ASIDE AND FORGOTTEN.

CAREFUL, SWEETHEART, THERE MAY BE SOME LOOSE RAZOR BLADES IN THERE.

WHAT'S THIS, POPPY?

IT WAS MY COMBAT INFANTRYMAN'S BADGE.

THAT'S AN AWARD FROM THE ARMY. I'D WONDERED WHERE IT WAS.

DID THE SOLDIERS AT YOUR WORK GIVE IT TO YOU?

THE MEMORIES FLOODED BACK.

NO, HONEY. BEFORE THE WAR IN VIETNAM THERE WAS A WAR IN A PLACE CALLED KOREA.

OH, FOR WHEN YOU WERE IN THE ARMY? WHAT DOES IT MEAN?

"WHAT DOES IT MEAN?"

POPPY?

I REMEMBER THE FREEZING COLD. MOST OF ALL I REMEMBER THE COLD. THE FROZEN TRENCHES, WORN SMOOTH BY HUNDREDS OF COMBAT BOOTS OVER MONTHS OF SEESAW FIGHTING. I WAS YOUNG, CHERRY, AND SCARED AS HELL.

LT? BATTALION SAYS THE CHINESE ARE MASSING FOR A PUSH. THEY SAY THEY'LL TRY TO REINFORCE US ASAP.

DON'T HOLD YOUR BREATH, NEITHAMMER, WE'RE NOT GOING TO GET JACK-SHIT FROM BATTALION.

I HAD BEEN OVER THERE A LITTLE OVER THREE WEEKS AND THEY SENT ME TO THE PERIMETER NORTH OF PUSAN, COMPANY CLERK FOR HEAD-QUARTERS AND HEADQUARTERS C.O.

DID YOU GET SGT. HAYES TO CHECK YOU OUT ON THE WATER-COOLED LIKE I TOLD YOU, NEITHAMMER?

YESSIR, BUT I'M AFRAID I CAN'T HIT THE BROAD SIDE OF A BARN.

WELL, IF PUSH COMES TO SHOVE YOU CAN FEED. NOW YOU'D BETTER GET SOME SLEEP WHILE YOU CAN. YOU'LL NEED ALL YOU CAN GET.

LIEUTENANT...I...

YOU'LL DO FINE, SON. YOU'LL DO FINE.

THANK YOU, SIR.

I HAD BEEN TRAINED AS A COMPANY CLERK, BUT EVEN THE ARMY'S INCESSANT PREOCCUPATION WITH PAPERWORK TAKES A BACK SEAT WHEN SURVIVAL IS AT STAKE. WE SPENT EVERY WAKING MOMENT SCRATCHING IN THE FROZEN GROUND, DEEPENING OUR POSITIONS...

...DISTRIBUTING OUR DWINDLING SUPPLY OF AMMUNITION ALONG THE LINE...

...AND SHIVERING. WE ALL HAD A SENSE OF IMPENDING DOOM.

NEITHAMMER, TELL LT THE PATROL IS COMING IN.

CHICKEN --

NO COUNTER-SIGN. THE TROOPS MOVED TOWARD US AT A LOW CROUCH, MOONLIGHT REFLECTING OFF THEIR STEEL POTS.

CHICKEN! DAMN IT!

MY GUTS KNOTTED AS THE TROOPER OPENED UP ON OUR PATROL.

AAAAAAHHHH! POST THREE! POST THREE!

SUDDENLY THE ENTIRE PERIMETER OPENED UP IN A FURIOUS FIREFIGHT.

POW POW POW POW POW

PA-DOW PA-DOW PA-DOW

THABOOM BBBBBAP

IT WAS OVER IN LESS THAN THIRTY SECONDS.

MY GOD! MY GOD!

THEY WERE CHINESE IN U.S. ARMY UNIFORMS. IT WAS CLEAR THAT THE PATROL HAD MET WITH TRAGEDY.

BUSTER BROWN, GET FIRST SQUAD TOGETHER. WE GOTTA GO AFTER THEM.

LT'S AT BATTALION, SARGE. YOU CAN'T LEAD A SQUAD INTO THE "Z" WITHOUT AUTHORIZATION.!

THOSE ARE MY PEOPLE OUT THERE. EVERY MINUTE COUNTS! WE DON'T HAVE TIME TO WAIT FOR THE BRASS TO MAKE UP THEIR MINDS.

I'M WITH YOU, SARGE.

ALL THE CORPORAL COULD FIND WERE FIVE MEMBERS OF THE FIRST SQUAD TO ACCOMPANY HIM AND SERGEANT GRINDLE INTO THE DMZ.

NEITHAMMER, AS SOON AS WE LEAVE, GET ON THE FIELD PHONE AND ALERT BATTALION. WE'LL BE BACK AS SOON AS WE CAN. PASSWORD "CHICKEN." COUNTERSIGN, "FEED."

I--GOOD LUCK.

CORPORAL, TAKE POINT.

WE RAN BELT AFTER BELT OF AMMO THROUGH THE MACHINE GUN. THE FIRE CUT THROUGH THE HORDE OF CHARGING CHINESE LIKE A SCYTHE THROUGH WHEAT.

WAVE AFTER WAVE NEARLY REACHED US, BUT WERE CUT DOWN. THE DEAD WERE PILED THREE FEET DEEP WHERE THEY FELL.

MORE AMMO, DAMN IT! MORE AMMO!

BUT THEY TOOK THEIR TOLL ON OUR SIDE, TOO. I HAD TO SCRAMBLE OVER THE BODIES OF MY FRIENDS TO REACH THE AMMUNITION BUNKER.

I HARDLY FELT THE EXPLOSION THAT BURIED ME.

THA BOOM

IRONICALLY, BEING BURIED UNDER THE COLLAPSED BUNKER SAVED MY LIFE AS THE CHINESE OVERRAN OUR POSITION.